Halfway
to Harmony

ALSO BY BARBARA O'CONNOR

Beethoven in Paradise

Me and Rupert Goody

Moonpie and Ivy

Fame and Glory in Freedom, Georgia

Taking Care of Moses

How to Steal a Dog

Greetings from Nowhere

The Small Adventure of Popeye and Elvis

The Fantastic Secret of Owen Jester

On the Road to Mr. Mineo's

Wish

Wonderland

BARBARA O'CONNOR

Halfway to Harmony

SQUARE
FISH

FARRAR STRAUS GIROUX

New York

SQUARE
FISH

An imprint of Macmillan Publishing Group, LLC
120 Broadway, New York, NY 10271 • mackids.com

Square Fish and the Square Fish logo are trademarks of Macmillan and
are used by Farrar Straus Giroux under license from Macmillan.

Our books may be purchased in bulk for promotional, educational, or
business use. Please contact your local bookseller or the Macmillan Corporate
and Premium Sales Department at (800) 221-7945 ext. 5442 or
by email at MacmillanSpecialMarkets@macmillan.com.

The Library of Congress has cataloged the hardcover edition as follows:
Names: O'Connor, Barbara, author.
Title: Halfway to Harmony / Barbara O'Connor.
Description: First edition. | New York: Farrar Straus Giroux Books for
Young Readers, 2021. | Audience: Ages 8–12. | Audience: Grades 4–6. |
Summary: Ten-year-old Walter Tipple is grieving his beloved older brother,
Tank, when a sassy girl named Posey moves in next door and
Banjo, a hot-air balloonist, sets the pair on an adventure.
Identifiers: LCCN 2020013648 | ISBN 9780374314453 (hardcover)
Subjects: CYAC: Friendship—Fiction. | Family life—Georgia—Fiction. | Hot-air
balloons—Fiction. | Death—Fiction. | Brothers—Fiction. | Georgia—Fiction.
Classification: LCC PZ7.O217 Hal 2021 | DDC [Fic]—dc23
LC record available at https://lccn.loc.gov/2020013648

Originally published in the United States by Farrar Straus Giroux
First Square Fish edition, 2022
Book designed by Aurora Parlagreco
Square Fish logo designed by Filomena Tuosto
Printed in the United States of America by LSC Communications,
Harrisonburg, Virginia.

ISBN 978-1-250-82106-5 (paperback)
5 7 9 10 8 6

AR: 5.0

For Amanda, with love

Halfway to Harmony

ONE

The night that Posey and Evalina moved to Harmony, Georgia, Walter Tipple had that dream again.

The one about his birthday.

Mama and Daddy are standing nearby, waiting for him to blow out the candles.

Eleven of them.

Everyone sings "Happy Birthday," but suddenly the screen door bursts open and in steps Walter's brother, Tank, in his army uniform.

He throws his arms out and says, "Look who's back!" while everyone stares, wide-eyed and gape-mouthed, like they've just seen a ghost.

Which, of course, they have.

The candles drip wax onto the buttercream frosting that Mama makes so good.

And then it happens.

Every single time Walter has that dream.

The ghost that is Tank takes off his army hat, plunks it down on Walter's head, and says, "Blow out them candles, little man, and I'll show you my world." He slaps Walter on the back and adds, "But you gotta blow 'em *all* out. First try. No cheating."

He grins that grin of his with the chipped front tooth.

Then he crosses his arms and taps his foot and says, "I ain't got all day."

So Walter looks down at those eleven candles, takes a deep breath . . .

. . . and wakes up.

Every single time.

The night that Evalina and Posey moved to Harmony, Walter had sat on the edge of the bed after that dream with his heart racing.

Then he'd heard a car bouncing and squeaking up the gravel road toward Ernest and Nadine's old tumble-down house next door.

He got out of bed and padded to the window, the

wide plank floor cool under his bare feet. The full moon glowed over the yard, making the clothesline cast an eerie shadow, like a long black snake that slithered through the garden and over the lawn chair where Daddy sometimes napped in the afternoon.

By the light of the moon, Walter saw Evalina's car pulling a trailer piled high with cardboard boxes. A washing machine. A mattress.

He hadn't seen Posey or her scruffy little dog, Porkchop, sitting in the front seat beside Evalina.

But the next day, he had done what Mama asked him to and run up to that old house with a jar of her bread-and-butter pickles. He stood on the wooden porch with half the boards missing and started counting to ten to calm his nerves before knocking on the door. But he had only gotten to six when a skinny, scabby-kneed girl came busting out onto the porch, followed by a small, yapping dog.

"Can't you read?" the girl hollered.

Walter nearly fell backward into the prickly bushes along the porch. And just when he thought his beating heart might come to a screeching halt, that girl stuck her face up close to his and said, "I suppose you can't talk, neither."

"Um . . ." Walter said, looking down at the pickle jar.

"Stick out your tongue," the girl snapped.

So, of course, that is exactly what Walter did.

He stuck out his tongue.

That was when Evalina came out onto the porch and said, "Good gravy and green beans, Posey. What you doing to that boy?"

"Checking to see if he can hear me, 'cause he sure can't read." Posey jabbed a finger at the sign nailed on the porch railing:

NO SOLICITORS

That sign had been there as long as Walter could remember and he *still* didn't know what solicitors were. He'd always figured it meant any human being who was breathing because Ernest and Nadine hadn't wanted *anybody* to set foot on their property. They stayed inside that falling-down house the livelong day, only opening the door every now and then to shoo cats out of their weed-filled yard.

Then one day Nadine died and three days later Ernest died. Not long after that, Mama heard somebody at the post office say that their daughter from Tennessee was coming to live in their old house.

Evalina.

Mama hadn't heard that Evalina had a skinny, scabby-kneed daughter named Posey and a yapping little dog named Porkchop.

Which was why it had come as a bit of a shock to Walter to find himself on their porch with a jar of pickles and that girl glaring at him and her dog snapping and snarling.

After he got over the shock, he took a good hard look at Posey and felt his spirits lift a little.

Right there in the middle of Posey's left cheek was a large heart-shaped birthmark.

Deep dark brown against her pale, freckled skin.

The instant Walter saw that birthmark, he began to think that maybe he and Posey were destined to be kindred spirits, bound together by the misfortune of being an easy target.

Walter had a lifetime of experience in being an easy target.

He was a quiet, timid, pigeon-toed boy with a lazy eye that never seemed to want to look where the other eye was looking.

Such boys were easy targets for the sharp-tongued kids in Harmony.

Now here was this girl with a heart-shaped birthmark on her cheek who was surely going to be an easy target, too.

Walter had waited his whole life for a kindred spirit and now here she was.

True, she seemed a little wild, wagging her finger at him and going on about that sign on the porch railing.

But then, Walter figured, beggars can't be choosers when it comes to kindred spirits.

He handed Evalina the jar of pickles, and that little dog snarled and snapped at his ankles, making him jump down off the porch, landing in the red dirt yard with a *thud*.

"Hush up, Porkchop," Posey said, holding the dog by his collar. She peered down at Walter and said, "He only bites if I tell him to."

Walter looked up at the dog and felt his mouth drop open in surprise.

That scruffy little dog only had three legs!

Two in the front and one in the back.

Posey must've seen Walter's surprise, because she said, "You gotta be tough when you look like ol' Porkchop here. He's a scrapper." She jabbed a thumb at herself and added, "Like me."

When he headed back home that day, Walter felt a little lighter. Maybe this summer was going to get better. The Tipples lived so far from town that Walter had never had anyone but Tank to hang out with. Now that Tank was gone, he spent every day alone.

His mind whirled with images of him and Posey having a grand old time together.

Looking for salamanders under the rotten logs down by the river.

Maybe adding a second story to the fort he and Tank had built way back in the woods behind a pile of termite-riddled lumber that used to be somebody's barn.

But later that night, Walter felt that familiar Mr. Doubt come creeping back, turning him into his worry-filled self again. He thought about Posey pointing at that NO SOLICITORS sign and squinting right up in his face so bossy and all.

He was starting to realize that Posey was probably one of those kids who had perfected the fine art of bully-thwarting.

He'd bet anything that when summer was over, she'd march herself right into Harmony Elementary School and dare those kids to laugh at her just by sending them a glare as mighty as any laser.

She'd probably snatch fish sticks right off the plates of first-graders at lunch or dare the third-graders to touch her birthmark and then charge them a quarter if they did.

Yep. Posey was a bully-thwarter the way that he, Walter Tipple, could never be.

She and that dog, Porkchop, were tough, the way that he, Walter Tipple, would never be.

By the time he fell asleep that night, Mr. Doubt had stepped aside and Mr. Disappointment had settled in. A bully-thwarter like Posey wouldn't want to hang out with a loser like him.

But then, the very next day, something happened that told Walter that fate might finally be on his side, sending him the kindred spirit he'd been waiting for, after all.

Because the very next day, when he and Posey and Porkchop were pushing their way through tangled pricker bushes and climbing over fallen trees in the dense woods beside the river, they found a dead man.

TWO

The morning after Walter delivered Mama's pickles to Evalina and Posey, he splashed cold water on his face, trying to clear his head of that dream he kept having. The one about his birthday with Tank telling him, "Blow out them candles, little man, and I'll show you my world."

At breakfast, Mama shuffled around the kitchen in her bathrobe and slippers, her face lined with the sadness that had been written on it every minute of every day for the last six months.

She dropped into the kitchen chair across from Walter and pushed a cereal box toward him. Walter sighed. He sure did miss that French toast and those blueberry pancakes she used to make for him and Tank.

Walter looked over at Tank's empty seat at the table and could practically hear him going on and on about Mama's cooking the way he used to, making her face light up and sending her back to the stove to cook some more.

Now silence settled over the little kitchen except for the sound of the leaky faucet dripping onto the pile of dirty dishes in the sink.

Mama stared out the window.

Walter stirred his cereal, feeling invisible.

"When's Daddy coming home?" he asked.

Mama took a sip of coffee and shrugged. "Soon," she said.

"How soon?"

"He'll be home for your birthday, for sure."

Good, Walter thought. Only about two more weeks.

Walter's daddy drove a truck for the lumber company and was sometimes gone for weeks at a time, leaving Walter and his mama here in the quiet emptiness without Tank.

Sometimes Walter imagined that he heard the sound of his brother's work boots on the worn oak floors.

His off-key singing drifting from his bedroom.

His corny jokes that made Mama laugh.

Walter set his bowl of soggy cereal on the floor for the cats and went out back to the barn. He pulled open both doors and stepped inside, peering into the darkness and breathing in the smell of damp earth and old wood. Motor oil and gasoline. He opened the door of Tank's shiny black pickup truck and climbed into the driver's seat, shut the door, and whispered, "Hey, Tank." He ran his hand along the polished chrome around the speedometer and the gauges. He pictured Tank here, vacuuming and polishing and buffing until everything about his beloved truck was perfect.

Walter put his cheek against the seat and took a deep breath. He was pretty sure he could still smell the faint hint of Tank's aftershave that hovered there.

Walter opened the glove box and felt the familiar stab at the sight of Tank's things.

A small canvas pouch filled with quarters.

A deck of cards covered with Tank's greasy fingerprints.

A pair of sunglasses.

A picture of a girl Tank used to date, sitting on the back of his truck. A heart drawn around her face with a red marker.

Walter took out the truck keys on the key chain with

Born to Be Wild stamped in the metal. He put the key in the ignition, like he had done every day since Tank left.

Like he had promised he would.

"Just let her run a few minutes every day," Tank had told him. Then, with a wink, he added, "Keep her all warmed up for when I get home."

In that dream Walter kept having, when the ghost of his brother shows up, nobody moves. Not even Walter. But in real life, he would've dashed over there and hugged his brother. He'd have been so happy that Tank had come home after all, even though that sad-faced army man from Fort Benning had come by the house six months ago and told them Tank wasn't ever coming home from the war he'd been fighting in overseas.

But Walter was still keeping his promise. That truck had been Tank's pride and joy, bought with money he'd earned whacking weeds and blowing leaves and digging fence-post holes every day after school. Now Walter was going to keep the truck warmed up and shiny and polished just the way Tank liked it. He was going to keep the windows perfectly clean. The silver hood ornament gleaming. The hubcaps shining like mirrors.

He turned the key and the engine started with a roar. Tank's favorite country music station blasted on. Some guy singing about putting money in the jukebox and slow-dancing until closing time.

Walter put his hands on the steering wheel and pretended to drive.

With the windows down and the warm Georgia air swirling around inside.

Tank used to let Walter drive sometimes. In cow pastures or plowed-up bean fields or big empty parking lots. The last time Walter drove the truck was one night in the parking lot of Oak Grove Methodist Church. Walter could barely reach the gas pedal as he craned his neck to see out into the darkness. They had whooped and hollered and Tank had told him about girls and high school and parties late at night out by the water tower. The one with HARMONY painted on it in red. Then on the way home, Tank had told Walter how he was going to join the army and get the heck out of Harmony, Georgia.

All the joy from earlier in the evening had come crashing down on Walter when he heard that.

"But where you gonna go?" he had asked with a lump in his throat so big he could barely get the words out.

"I don't know yet," Tank said. "Just need to spread

my wings a little, you know? Harmony, Georgia, ain't nothing but a dot in the universe."

"What about me?" Walter asked in a small, wavering voice. "If you're spreading your wings, what am I supposed to do?"

Tank punched him on the arm. "You gotta serve your time, little man. You gotta serve your time."

"What does that mean?"

"Finish school. Mow some lawns. Kiss some girls." Tank winked at Walter. "You gotta grow wings before you can spread 'em."

Then they had driven home in silence, Tank with his arm draped out the window and Walter thinking about serving his time.

Now he was sitting here in the pickup truck, feeling sorry for himself. He reached into the glove box and took out an envelope. He looked down at his own name and address scribbled in Tank's messy handwriting.

Walter just couldn't bring himself to open that envelope. He had saved Tank's other letters and read them countless times. But this one had come two days after that army man had told them Tank was never coming home.

Was this letter the same as the others that Walter kept tucked in his dresser drawer?

16

Telling him about his brother's exciting life far away from home.

Making it sound so good.

Making it sound like he didn't miss Harmony one bit.

Or would this letter say something different?

Would this letter finally say how much Tank missed Harmony?

And would this letter finally say he was sorry he hadn't come home to tell Walter goodbye before he went overseas like he promised he would?

Thinking about those things made Walter's insides tumble with anger and then the heavy burden of guilt hung over him. He didn't want to be mad at the brother he was missing so much. Being mad at Tank felt just plain wrong. But anger and grief wrestled each other inside him nearly every minute of the day.

Walter turned the truck off and put the key and the envelope back into the glove box and whispered, "Bye, Tank."

He shut the truck door and wiped a smudge off the handle with the bottom of his T-shirt, closed the barn doors, and ran smack dab into Posey.

THREE

"Evalina told me to give you your pickle jar back but I need it." Posey was wearing dirty rubber boots that came clear up to her knees. Porkchop trotted along behind her, hopping up and down with his one back leg. His brown-and-white fur stuck up every which way and his tail waved in the air like a flag.

Walter blinked. "Um . . ."

"I found some more jars in your shed," she said, motioning toward the tiny shed by the garden. She held up a plastic bag, making the jars inside clatter.

"Isn't Evalina your mama?" Walter asked.

"Yep."

"Then why do you call her Evalina?"

"'Cause that's her name," Posey said. Then she

marched across the yard toward the road with Pork-chop racing ahead.

"Hey!" Walter called after her.

She stopped clomping and turned around.

Cocked her head.

Lifted her eyebrows.

"What are you gonna do with those jars?" Walter asked.

Posey looked him up and down long enough to make him shift nervously from one foot to the other.

"Catch minnows," she said. "Well, probably not *real* minnows. Unless there's carp in that river. Any carp in that river?"

"Some," Walter said. "But mostly trout and catfish."

"*Real* minnows are carp," Posey said. "I know that because I've read *Nuggets of Knowledge* four times and I have practically a photographic memory so I remember nearly everything I read in there." She shifted the bag from one hand to the other. "You ever read that book?"

Walter shook his head.

"It's my favorite. I got it at the Goodwill in Tennessee where we used to live. I had a ton of books but Evalina made me leave most of them behind so I just brought my favorites. I've got one about teaching dogs to do tricks. Watch this."

She made a circle with her hand and Porkchop laid down and rolled over.

"Where are you going to catch minnows?" Walter asked.

"Duh. Like I said, the river."

Walter shook his head. "Good luck."

"What's that supposed to mean?"

He shrugged. He had lived here beside the Chattahoochee River his whole life. He knew the best place to catch minnows was in the clear water of the creeks that flowed through the woods.

"Means you'll find more minnows in the creeks than the river," he said.

"You a minnow expert?"

"No, but . . ."

"Bet you didn't know that nugget of knowledge about minnows being carp," Posey said.

Then she and Porkchop headed off up the middle of the road, those jars clattering with every clomp, Posey calling behind her, "You coming or not?"

FOUR

By the time Walter caught up with Posey, he was out of breath, sweat running down his neck in the Georgia heat.

The whole time they made their way up the narrow path toward the creek, jumping over gullies, climbing over fallen trees, stepping carefully around pricker bushes, Posey jabbered nonstop.

She told Walter about her friend Lettie back in Tennessee who had sleeping sickness.

"Just fell asleep right in the middle of dinner," Posey said. "One time, she fell asleep standing up! I kid you not."

She told him how her daddy got a job as a traveling salesman when she was a baby.

"Problem was, he just kept on traveling and never came back," she said. "I used to think he left me 'cause of this." She pointed to the heart-shaped birthmark on her face. "But Evalina's told me about a hundred times to hush up saying that, so I guess I don't think it anymore."

Then she told Walter how the preacher at Spiny Grove Baptist Church in Tennessee had told her that the birthmark was a direct result of being kissed by an angel.

"I happen to know that's a bunch of bull," Posey said. "Angels don't have time to kiss all the babies in the world. Besides, more like getting kicked by the devil, if you ask me."

On and on she went.

She told him about how Porkchop had just shown up on their front porch one night during a thunderstorm.

"He was practically bald from the mange and covered with ticks," she said. "He was nothing but skin and bones. When I let him inside, he jumped up on the kitchen table and snatched Evalina's porkchop right off her plate."

22

"Is that why you named him Porkchop?" Walter asked.

"Well, duh. Anyways, Evalina pitched a fit and wanted to take him to the pound, but I pitched a fit right back. I knew he needed me, seeing as how he's only got three legs. He looks different and, believe me, I know how *that* feels."

Walter wished he could ask her if kids said mean things about her birthmark, but even if he'd had the nerve (which he didn't), she wouldn't stop talking long enough for him to say diddly.

"And *then*," she went on, "it was kind of a stroke of good luck when Ernest and Nadine died 'cause we got a whole house for free. Ernest and Nadine were my grand-daddy and grandmama, you know."

Walter nodded.

"I know it probably sounds mean, what I just said about them dying," Posey continued, "but I never met 'em and Evalina told me they were not very nice. She used to say we weren't never coming to Harmony but she changed her mind 'cause of the free house."

When a small black snake slithered across the path in front of them, she said, "I bet you didn't know that the longest snake on record was thirty feet long and weighed three hundred pounds." She poked at the snake with the toe of her boot before it disappeared under a mound of rotting leaves. "Another nugget of knowledge," she added.

They were almost to the creek when Posey hollered, "Wait!"

Walter stopped.

"Look!" Posey pointed into the woods.

Walter looked. "What?"

"Hold on to your skivvies 'cause you will *not* believe this." Posey motioned for him to follow her through a tangle of chokeweeds where Porkchop was sniffing around like crazy and whining.

"Look!" Posey said again.

Walter looked.

Poking out of the dense shrubs were feet.

Two feet, to be exact.

One foot wore a sneaker with a hole in the toe.

The other foot was bare. Bruised and scratched.

"Who is that?" Posey whispered.

Walter felt sick, his stomach churning, but he couldn't take his eyes off those feet.

Posey carefully set the bag of jars down and picked up a stick. She put a finger to her lips and went, "Shhh."

Then she used the stick to push the bushes out of the way.

There, slumped against a sweet gum tree, was a dead man.

FIVE

"Whoa!" Posey stood there with the stick in her hand, holding the bushes back and staring at the dead man.

Porkchop whined.

Walter froze.

He couldn't move.

He couldn't talk.

His head spun and his legs shook.

He closed his eyes. "What's wrong with him?" he whispered.

"Looks dead to me."

"Dead?"

"Dead as a doornail," Posey said. "You know him?"

Walter did *not* want to look at that man's face.

Looking at his feet was bad enough. Slowly he opened one eye and forced himself to glance at the man. Then he opened his other eye and took a deep breath.

The dead man had a very bushy mustache that turned up at the ends like a smile. His face was covered with scratches. Over one eye was an angry red lump the size of an egg. His hair was kind of wild looking, full of leaves and hanging clear down to his shoulders. His plaid shirt and denim overalls were ripped and streaked with mud. One hand loosely clutched a clump of sweet gum leaves while the other lay limply beside him.

Walter took another deep breath and held it for a minute, trying to get his thumping heart to slow down. He was pretty sure he knew nearly everyone in Harmony, but he most definitely did not know this man.

"Well?" Posey said.

Walter shook his head. "Never seen him before in my life." He looked at Posey, who was still holding the bushes back with the stick. "What should we do?" he asked.

Posey tossed the stick into the woods and let the bushes flap back against the man with a *thwap*.

She grinned at Walter. "Call 911!" she said. "I've always wanted to call 911."

Call 911? Walter had never really thought about it before, but now that Posey said it, he realized he had probably always wanted to call 911, too.

He looked at Posey with new admiration. His very first day with this girl and they were calling 911!

"Let's go!" Posey said, whistling for Porkchop and hurrying up the path with her boots clomping and her thin hair flying.

Walter hurried after them.

But they didn't get far.

Because suddenly, in the quiet of the Georgia woods, came the sound of a moan.

SIX

Walter stopped.

Posey stopped.

Porkchop stopped.

There it was again.

A moan.

If Walter had been alone, he knew exactly what he would've done.

Run like crazy.

But with Posey standing beside him, running didn't seem like the thing to do.

So he just stood there and waited.

Porkchop cocked his head and let out a low growl.

Posey went, "Shhh," and motioned for Walter and Porkchop to follow her back to where those two feet stuck out of the bushes. She squatted on the ground and motioned for Walter to do the same.

"I think he's alive!" Posey whispered.

Walter nodded.

The sound of his own heartbeat pounded in his ears.

He held his breath as Posey slowly pushed the bushes aside.

There was that man.

His eyes were closed.

One hand still clutched the sweet gum leaves.

But the other hand began to twitch.

His eyelids began to flutter.

And then another moan.

Porkchop barked.

Suddenly both of the man's eyes popped open and stared up at the canopy of trees overhead.

A gravelly voice made Walter jump.

"Am I dead?" the man asked, still staring at the sky.

Posey went, "*Pfft*," and said, "No deader than me."

The man's eyes jerked wildly around, searching the branches above him, then lowering slowly until they focused on Posey, who was sitting on the ground holding the bushes aside.

"You an angel?" he whispered.

"Do I look like an angel?" She jerked a thumb toward Walter. "Does *he* look like an angel?"

The man closed his eyes and moaned again. "Then where in tarnation am I?"

"A long way from heaven, right, Walter?" Posey poked Walter with her elbow.

Walter looked at the man, so scratched up and dirty, and decided he deserved a proper answer to an honest question.

"You're in the woods beside the Chattahoochee River in Harmony, Georgia," he said.

The man coughed a rattly cough and winced. "Am I in one piece? I'm scared to look."

Posey squinted at him. "As far as I can tell, yes, you are. Walter, does he look like he's in one piece to you?"

Walter took a quick inventory of the man. Two arms. Two hands. Two legs. Two feet. His eyes lingered for a minute on that one bruised and scratched bare foot.

"Yep," Walter said. "Missing a shoe, though."

The man lifted his head and stared at his foot as if he'd forgotten he had one.

"Dang it!" he said. "That was a perfectly good shoe."

Porkchop walked slowly around the man, sniffing and growling.

"Will somebody get that mutt away from me?" the man said.

Posey called Porkchop, who trotted to her and sat, his wagging tail making swishing noises in the dried leaves.

"I'm sorry to have to tell you this, mister," Posey said, "but you don't look too good."

The man scowled. "You wouldn't look too good yourself, missy, if you fell out of the sky."

"Ha!" Posey said. "Fell out of the sky? That's a bunch of baloney."

Walter looked up at the trees overhead. Sunlight filtered through them, leaving streaks of golden light dancing among the branches. Had this man really fallen out of the sky?

"You two just gonna sit there?" the man snapped. "I'm in a bit of a pickle here, in case you haven't noticed. I think my ankle's broke."

"You got a name?" Posey asked.

"'Course I got a name."

Posey stood up and with a big, dramatic toss of her hand, released the branches she had been holding back, letting them whack that man right in the face.

"Hey!" he hollered, making Porkchop bark.

Posey jammed her fists into her waist and yelled into the bushes: "Seems to me like somebody in such a pickle would consider being a tad *nicer*."

"Okay, okay." The man's voice traveled through the bushes. "Banjo! My name's Banjo! Now y'all gonna help me get outta here or not?"

Posey pulled the branches away from the man's face. "Banjo?"

"What kinda name is that?" Walter asked.

The man let out a big heaving sigh. "I will most definitely work on being *nice*. But right now, I'm not exactly in the mood. Are y'all gonna help me or not?"

Posey looked at Walter. "Should we help him?"

"Well, um, yeah!" Walter said. "We gotta help him. Call 911?"

Posey nodded. "Yep, 911."

SEVEN

The EMTs finally got Banjo out of the woods on a stretcher and were loading him into an ambulance, when Evalina hurried after him, waving a paper bag.

"Wait! Stop!" she called. "That poor man needs some food."

She set the paper bag carefully on the stretcher beside Banjo. He opened his eyes and looked at Evalina.

"Sweet glory hallelujah," he said. "I *am* dead!"

Evalina chuckled. "You're looking a little rough, but you are most definitely not dead."

"Then why is there an angel standing over me?"

Evalina blushed, and then Posey piped in, "He thought I was an angel, too. The man is some kinda kook, if you ask me."

"Nobody's asking you," Evalina snapped.

Banjo held up the paper bag and waved it feebly. "This!" he said. "Only an angel would give me this."

Evalina flapped her hand and said, "Aw, now, that's nothing but a couple of liver-mush sandwiches."

"Liver mush?" Banjo said. "My personal favorite. Delivered to me by a beautiful angel. Who would've thought this day would turn out so fine?"

Banjo took a deep sniff of the paper bag and closed his eyes with a contented sigh. Then he looked at Evalina and said, "I'll be back, Miss Angel. I got some unfinished business in them woods."

"What happened to you back there, anyway?" Evalina asked.

Banjo tipped an imaginary hat. "I'll tell you all about it when I return."

With that, Banjo disappeared inside the ambulance and Evalina, Posey, Porkchop, and Walter watched as it bounced down the gravel road and turned onto the main highway.

Walking home that afternoon, Walter thought about how yesterday had been boring and filled with the emptiness left by Tank, but today had been crazy and surprising and even a little fun.

When he got home, Mama was snapping green beans at the kitchen table and tossing them into a pot.

"What in the world's going on next door?" she asked.

Walter told her about the man who fell out of the sky.

"Fell out of the sky?" she said. "That's hogwash."

Snap.

Toss.

"That's what he told me and Posey," Walter said.

"Well, the man's either a nut or a liar, or both."

Snap.

Toss.

Walter sighed. Mama was always so grumpy lately. He wished he could remember some of those jokes that Tank used to tell, but he couldn't.

He went out to the barn and walked around Tank's truck, inspecting it, making sure everything was perfect.

No mouse droppings on the hood.

No cobwebs on the mirrors.

He took an old towel from a peach basket and polished fingerprints off the fender. Then he stepped back and admired the shiny truck.

Tank's best friend, Lester, had painted orange flames on the sides and a lightning bolt on the tailgate. Tank had put a sticker in the rear window that said *Bad to the Bone*, but Mama had pitched a fit and tried to take it off. The only part that was left was *the Bone*. Some girl's necklace hung from the rearview mirror. A gold chain with a rhinestone horseshoe.

Walter could practically see Tank sitting there behind the wheel. Sometimes it felt like just yesterday his brother had been driving his truck up and down Main Street with Walter beside him. That truck was fast and loud and made the old folks in Harmony scowl at them, which, of course, made Tank smile and wink at Walter.

Sometimes Tank let Walter come with him out to the water tower where his high school friends hung out in the evenings. Walter always watched Tank's every move. The way he fist-bumped the boys and sweet-talked the girls. One time, on the way home, Tank had poked Walter in the arm and said, "Ain't I Mr. Smooth?"

Walter would have given anything to be riding out to the water tower with Mr. Smooth again.

That night, Walter had the dream.

Same birthday cake.

Same people gathered around.

Those eleven candles dripping wax onto Mama's buttercream frosting.

Tank saying, "Blow out them candles, little man, and I'll show you my world."

Walter looking down at those candles and then, like always, he woke up.

EIGHT

Mama stood up from the lawn chair by the garden and said, "What in the world?"

Walter stopped picking cucumbers and stared.

A rusty pickup truck had turned off the highway and was chugging up the gravel road toward them, leaving a trail of black smoke behind it. The engine coughed and sputtered as the truck passed them and came to a stop in front of Evalina's house.

While Walter and Mama stared, the truck seemed to make one last gasp.

Cough out one last puff of smoke.

Shudder one last rattle.

The door of the truck squeaked open and the driver stepped out.

Banjo!

Walter recognized that twirly mustache right away. And even from over by the garden, he could see that big red lump over Banjo's eye. He could also see a blue cast on one foot and a pair of crutches.

"Who in the name of Jemima Jones is *that*?" Mama asked.

"It's Banjo!" Walter said. "That man who fell out of the sky."

Walter raced across the yard. "Banjo!" he called, waving his arms.

Banjo didn't look up. He hobbled up the side of the road on his crutches, muttering under his breath.

All of a sudden, Posey burst out of her screen door, followed by a yapping Porkchop. She jumped off the front porch, ran over to Banjo, and skidded to a stop, sending gravel tumbling into the drainage ditch that ran along the edge of the road.

Porkchop snarled and snapped at the air in front of Banjo, who stopped hobbling and waved a crutch in the air.

"Watch it, missy!" he hollered. "And get that three-legged fleabag away from me."

Posey motioned for Porkchop to sit, which he did, growling softly and keeping his gaze on Banjo.

Posey narrowed her eyes and looked Banjo up and down, from his stringy hair to the cast on his foot. "You don't look much better than you did yesterday," she said.

Banjo leaned on his crutches and scowled at her. "Look," he snapped. "Don't you know better than to pick a fight with a one-footed man? I'm not feeling very sociable right now." He looked forlornly down at his cast.

"What'd you come back here for?" Posey poked a finger at him. "And where do you live, anyway?"

Banjo lowered his bad foot to the ground and winced. "Gol-dern it, missy! Can't you see—"

"My *name* is Posey."

Banjo squinted at her. "That so?"

He looked over at Posey and Evalina's house. "Where's that angel lady?"

Posey rolled her eyes and let out a little puff of air that blew her thin hair off her forehead. "If you're talking about Evalina, I can guarantee you she's no angel."

Just then Evalina came out onto her porch, raising her eyebrows. "What's going on?" she asked.

Banjo stopped and stared dreamy-eyed up at her. He lifted one crutch off the ground and did a little half bow toward her.

"I am Jubilation T. Fairweather, otherwise known as Banjo, sending a most hearty greeting to you, the fairest angel these tired old eyes have ever had the good fortune to feast upon."

Posey made a gagging sound and said, "Oh, *puh-leeze!*"

Banjo hobbled toward Evalina with Walter, Posey, and Porkchop following him.

When he got to the porch, he dropped onto the bottom step with a grunt and said, "Allow me to explain my presence."

Posey cocked her head at Walter and said, "This oughta be good."

NINE

Posey and Walter sat on the steps and Evalina lowered herself onto the porch swing.

Banjo cleared his throat. "I'll give y'all the short version and save the long version for a starry night on that porch swing up yonder."

He looked at Evalina and winked, making Posey shake her head.

Banjo gave his mustache a twirl. "I'll begin the short version with the origin of my name, Banjo," he said. "I have five older brothers who were mean as snakes and picked on me every minute of the day." He stopped and ducked his head at Walter and Posey. "*Picked* on me," he said. "Banjo? Get it?"

Walter grinned. "Oh yeah! I get it! Picking on a banjo!"

Banjo chuckled. "My dear departed mama named me that." He put his hand over his heart. "May she rest in everlasting peace for all eternity."

Posey stared at Banjo with a most unimpressed look, but Evalina nodded and placed her hand over her heart, too, while pushing the swing with her bare foot on the warped boards of the porch.

"Anyway," Banjo continued, "them five mean brothers of mine stayed on the family farm over in Claxton. But me? I hightailed it outta there as soon as I was old enough to have a couple of nickels in my overalls, and have lived a life of blessed peace and solitude over in Pine Mountain ever since." He paused to look at each of them with an expression of proud contentment. "In a humble dwelling made with these very hands," he continued, waving his scratched-up hands in the air. "Not too far from this lovely abode, I might add."

Evalina chuckled, but Posey said, "Are you getting to the point anytime soon?"

Banjo gave his mustache another twirl and continued. "To keep my mind sharp and my hands busy, I have been working on a project that I call Banjo's Bodacious Adventure."

Walter widened his eyes and looked at Posey, but she examined her fingernails and faked a yawn.

"What's the bodacious adventure?" Walter asked.

"I'm glad you asked," Banjo said. He took a deep breath. "I have spent many a day making and perfecting the world's most beautiful and, I am certain, the world's fastest hot-air balloon."

Posey's mouth dropped open and she whirled around to look at Walter, whose mouth had dropped open, too.

"Whoa!" Walter said. Hot-air balloon? He felt excitement zipping and zapping through him. Never in his wildest dreams had he expected that.

"You heard me right," Banjo said. "The world's fastest hot-air balloon."

Posey lifted her eyebrows. "World's fastest?" she said.

Banjo cocked his head at her. "Why, is that doubt I see swirling around you?" He leaned forward and spoke softly. "Hear my story, Miss Posey, and you will shed your doubt like a snake sheds his skin." Then he sat up straight and lifted a finger in the air. "First," he continued, "I became a proud and valued member of the Macon County Hot-Air Balloon Society, where I learned everything there is to know about hot-air balloons. Then I made myself a balloon with a heavy-duty sewing machine I bought when a textile mill closed down near Atlanta. Every color of the rainbow with silver stars and golden moons. Assembled every piece of that balloon with love and care. I named my balloon *Starcatcher*." He clutched his heart and sighed. "I've been ticking off the days on my calendar until the Macon County Key Grab over in Oakley."

"What's a key grab?" Walter asked.

"A key grab, young man, is a competition in which hot-air balloons race to a very tall pole," Banjo explained. "On top of that pole are the keys to a shiny new pickup truck, which I, Jubilation T. Fairweather, am destined to win." He nodded knowingly at Walter. "Unfortunately, I have run into a slight obstacle to my destiny," he added, glancing down at the cast on his foot. "A most unfortunate accident occurred. I took my big, beautiful balloon out for a test ride. I drifted along up there in the Georgia sky and life was good, but in a blink the weather took a turn for the worse. A mighty gust of wind came out of nowhere and like to knocked me cross-eyed. And then that balloon began to drift toward the river."

Walter and Posey leaned in a little closer. Evalina sat still on the swing with her hands in her lap.

"Closer and closer it got to the river," Banjo said. "And *then*—" He stopped for a second or two and let the drama swirl around them a bit. "And *then*," he continued, "something went awry and that precious balloon of mine began to drop. Down, down, down toward the river. I watched that water get closer and closer and, try as I might, I was unable to control my beloved *Starcatcher*."

Banjo shook his head and let out a big sigh.

Walter waited.

Posey waited.

Evalina waited.

Porkchop thumped his tail against the porch steps.

"Now, I'm here to tell you that I am blessed with many fine talents, skills, and abilities," Banjo continued, "but swimming ain't one of them." He nodded slowly. "You heard correctly. I, Jubilation T. Fairweather, cannot swim."

Posey crossed her arms. "And?"

"I knew I had but two choices as that balloon drifted down toward the river," Banjo said.

Walter took a breath and held it, his eyes wide.

Posey bounced up and down. "*What* two choices?" she said.

Banjo looked at Posey.

Then at Walter.

Then up at Evalina.

"Jump or die," he said. "Jump or die."

Walter let his breath out with a *whoosh*.

Banjo nodded. "You heard me right. Jump or die."

"I don't get it," Posey said. "Seems to me like you'd die either way."

"Wrong." Banjo leaned closer to Posey. "I was quite certain I had a better chance of jumping into them woods and living to tell the tale than crashing into the river, where I would surely have perished, never to return to this blessed earth again."

"So what happened?" Walter asked.

"That balloon continued to drop," Banjo said. "Down, down, down."

"Holy cow," Walter said.

"Lordy May," Evalina said.

"So you jumped," Posey said.

Banjo winked at her. "That I did, Miss Posey. That I did."

He picked up a stick by the porch steps and used it to scratch an itch somewhere inside that big blue cast on his foot.

He smiled at Evalina. "Ain't it funny how things happen like that. One minute I'm preparing for the possibility of meeting Saint Peter at the pearly gates and the next thing I know an angel right here on earth is giving me liver-mush sandwiches."

"Oh, for crying out loud," Posey said. "You left out the best part of the story."

"And what might that be?" Banjo asked.

"Where's that balloon?"

Banjo jabbed a finger at Posey. "*That*, missy, is precisely why I have returned to this little slice of heaven." He swept his arms out with a flourish. "To find my balloon."

TEN

Banjo huffed and puffed and grunted and groaned as he and Walter and Posey made their way through the woods with Porkchop racing ahead on his three short legs. Every now and then they came to a fallen tree or a patch of brambles and Banjo let a few cusswords fly.

Walter walked slowly so as not to leave Banjo behind, but Posey charged ahead, following the narrow path they had used when they had come upon Banjo by the sweet gum tree. If they could find that exact spot, then maybe they could figure out which direction the balloon had continued in and how far it might have gone before it landed.

"Slow down, missy!" Banjo hollered.

"No!" Posey hollered back.

Banjo gave Walter a sympathetic look. "You sure got yourself one bossy girlfriend," he said, wiping sweat off the back of his neck with a dirty handkerchief.

"Um, she's not my girlfriend."

"That a fact?"

"Yessir."

"What in tarnation happened to that yappy little dog of hers? I ain't seen a three-legged dog since I used to hunt rabbits with my uncle Tater."

Before Walter could answer, Posey yelled from the woods, "Here it is!"

Walter raced ahead, with Banjo hobbling and wheezing behind him.

When Walter reached Posey, she nodded toward Porkchop, who was sniffing like crazy in the leaves and pine needles. "That's where Banjo landed." Then she pointed and said, "Pine Mountain is that way." She pointed in the opposite direction. "And the river is that way."

Walter squinted in the direction she pointed. "Are you sure? I thought Pine Mountain was that way."

Banjo suddenly arrived in the clearing, panting and grumbling.

Porkchop stopped sniffing and let out a deep-throated growl.

"Now hold on a gol-dern minute, you two," Banjo said. "Let me get my bearings. And keep that angry mutt away from me."

Posey crossed her arms. "Porkchop only bites when I tell him to," she said. "*And* geography happens to be one of my specialties."

Walter raised his eyebrows, and Banjo went, "Ha!"

"Do either one of y'all know what the geographical center of the United States is?" Posey asked.

Banjo looked at Walter. "Don't answer that," he said. "It's liable to be a trick question."

Posey put her arms straight down by her sides, lifted her chin, and said, "Lots of people think the geographical center of the United States is in the eastern part of Smith County, Kansas. Latitude 39 degrees, 50 minutes. Longitude 98 degrees, 35 minutes. Because there's a sign there that says it is." She looked smugly from Walter to Banjo. "But after Alaska became a state in 1959, the center is actually in South Dakota."

"Oh, good grief and grits," Banjo mumbled.

"*Nuggets of Knowledge?*" Walter asked.

Posey nodded. "Yep."

Banjo dropped his crutches and lowered himself to

the ground with a grunt, his now-dirty cast stretched out in front of him. "I hate to say it, son," he said to Walter, "but I think your friend is right. Pine Mountain is thata way. The river is thata way. So if y'all go on through them woods down yonder in that direction, I figure you should arrive at the area where my balloon oughta be in about a half hour or so."

Posey's face turned red and that heart-shaped birthmark grew deep dark purple. "You're out of your everloving mind if you think Walter and me are gonna traipse through those woods for half an hour to find your balloon," she said. "Right, Walter?"

Walter didn't want to be rude to Banjo, but he had to agree with Posey. Even though he wanted to find that balloon more than anything, leaving the path and traipsing through those thick woods to the river didn't sound like much fun. He nodded at Posey and gave Banjo an apologetic look.

"Besides," Walter said, "if that balloon landed in the river, it's liable to be halfway to Florida by now."

Banjo shook his head. "Then I don't know what this world is coming to when two able-bodied young folks can't help an injured and hobbling gentleman find his most treasured possession. His dream of a lifetime. The product of his blood, sweat, and tears for nigh on two years." He shook his head and looked sadly up at the sky. "Just when I thought I'd found two kind souls to help me fulfill my dream, reality comes crashing down around me. There is no goodness in this world. Just pain and misery."

A wave of guilt washed over Walter, but Posey gave the biggest eye roll he had ever seen. "Oh, give me a break," she said.

"Naw, now." Banjo flapped a hand at them. "I'll figure this out by myself. You two run along, and by the way, thanks for nothing."

"I never saw a grown man be such a big baby," Posey said. "I've got an idea how to find that balloon. Have fun at your pity party."

Then she turned and disappeared through the woods with Porkchop hop-trotting along behind her, leaving Walter and Banjo staring in confusion.

Walter felt a sudden swell of admiration for Posey. She wasn't going to let Banjo boss her around. He was pretty sure she was, indeed, a bully-thwarter. Walter made a promise to himself that by the time school started in mid-August, he was going to march right into

Harmony Elementary School and be a bully-thwarter, too.

Maybe.

But for now, he was going to help Banjo up off the ground and see what in the world Posey had in mind.

ELEVEN

Banjo's truck whirred and sputtered.

Whirred and sputtered.

It shook and squeaked and coughed thick black smoke out of the tailpipe.

Banjo cussed and called it names and banged the steering wheel with his fists.

But the truck wouldn't start.

Walter and Posey sat beside Banjo in the front seat, with Porkchop curled contentedly on Posey's lap.

"Well, that's just great," Posey said.

"How are we gonna look for the balloon now?" Walter asked.

Their plan had been to drive up Highway 14 along

the river and keep an eye out for Banjo's hot-air balloon.

Posey had drawn a map on a brown paper bag with
a blue crayon showing where she calculated the balloon
had most likely come down. And even though Banjo
had shaken his head and said, "Color me highly skeptical of those calculations," he had agreed to at least take
a drive.

But then the truck wouldn't start.

"Never fear, children," Banjo said. "Jubilation T.
Fairweather always has plan B."

Posey lifted her eyebrows. "Which is?"

"Well, um . . ." Banjo's eyes darted around and he
snapped his fingers. "Evalina!" He looked from Posey to
Walter and grinned.

"Evalina?" Posey said.

Banjo nodded. "Evalina. She has a car, does she
not?"

"Your point?"

"And she can drive, can she not?"

"Your point?"

"My *point*, missy, is that I would wager all the grits
in Georgia that Evalina would be delighted to help

yours truly get one step closer to fulfilling the dream of his bodacious adventure by driving us to look for my balloon. Then after I fix my truck, I'll scoop up my beloved *Starcatcher*."

"Oh, for crying out loud," Posey said. "I've lived with her my whole life, which is ten years, six months, two weeks, and about four days, and I can tell you now she will want no part of your bodacious adventure." Posey jerked a thumb toward her house. "That woman is no-nonsense with a capital *N*."

"Nonsense?" Banjo snapped. "That what you think this is? Nonsense? Okay, then me and Walter will find a way to continue my bodacious adventure." He poked Walter in the shoulder. "Right, son?"

"W-well, um, I—I—" Walter stuttered and stammered. He was fond of Banjo, of course. But he wasn't too sure about getting involved in his bodacious adventure without Posey. After all, Posey was the adventurous type, while he, Walter Tipple, most definitely was not.

Posey yanked the truck door open, let Porkchop jump out, then shut it with a dramatic slam. "Have fun!" she said. Then she marched across the yard with her chin in the air and her arms pumping, stomped up the porch steps, and disappeared inside the house with Porkchop.

Walter and Banjo sat in silence.

A fly buzzed frantically against the windshield inside the truck.

Banjo frowned. "Well, this is a fine predicament," he said.

Walter nodded. "Yessir."

"Got any ideas?"

"No, sir."

"Me neither."

They watched the fly continue to buzz against the windshield and then finally zoom out the open window beside Walter.

The silence blended with the warm summer air and settled over them like a blanket.

Then, much to Walter's surprise, Banjo's head dropped back against the seat and he began to snore.

Deep, gurgly snores followed by puffs of air that moved his mustache ever so slightly.

Walter slowly opened the truck door, closed it with a soft push, and headed for home.

TWELVE

When Walter got home, he decided to go sit in Tank's room for a while like he often did. Sometimes he could practically see Tank in there, tossing a baseball from hand to hand or talking to some girl on the phone.

But when he opened the door and stepped inside, he nearly died of shock and horror at the sight of the room that used to belong to his brother.

The shelf where Tank's football trophies had been was empty. The top of his brother's scuffed-up desk that had been littered with motorcycle magazines and empty potato chip bags was bare.

Walter's stomach squeezed tight and his legs felt shaky.

He stared at the bed where Tank would sometimes

sleep the day away while their daddy banged on the door every hour or so. Instead of a jumble of sheets and smooshed-up pillows, there was a flowery quilt with a crocheted afghan folded neatly at the end of the bed.

Instead of the blanket that Tank had nailed over his window to keep out the light, there were lacy white curtains.

Walter closed his eyes and took a deep breath. Then he put his hand on the knob of the closet door and counted to three:

One.

Two.

Three.

He opened the door and peered inside.

Empty.

No football jerseys.

No fake leather jacket.

No muddy work boots.

Walter felt a little sick.

Just two days ago he had sat on Tank's unmade bed and held Tank's trophies and even put on Tank's jacket.

And now?

Poof!

Everything was gone.

His mother had taken away everything that was left of Tank.

Walter hurried out to the barn to sit in Tank's truck. He started to climb inside, but something caught his eye in the corner of the barn by the lawn mower.

A stack of cardboard boxes with *Tank* written on the sides with black marker.

Walter felt anger swirl around him and then hit him hard, like a punch. How could his mother put Tank's things away in boxes like that? How could she erase Tank right out of the house like he'd never even lived there?

He climbed into the truck and whispered, "Hey, Tank." Then he let the engine run while he shuffled Tank's cards and counted the quarters in the canvas bag. He jiggled the *Born to Be Wild* key chain and put on Tank's sunglasses. He gave himself a thumbs-up in the rearview mirror the way Tank used to, but he didn't look cool like his brother had.

He took the envelope out of the glove box and looked down at his name and address scrawled in Tank's scribbly writing and felt that mixed-up tangle of anger and sadness.

Why had Tank wanted to leave Harmony so bad?

Had his life in the army really been so much better?

And how could he have gone to fight in a war overseas like he did without even coming home to say goodbye to Walter, who loved him so much?

And the question that stabbed at Walter the most was this: Had Tank planned on ever coming back to Harmony?

Walter held the envelope in his shaking hands and wondered if he should open it. Maybe this last letter said the things Walter wanted it to.

About missing Harmony.

About wanting to come home.

But what if it didn't?

He tossed the envelope back in the glove box and put his hands on the steering wheel. He pretended he was big and strong like Tank and not small and puny like he really was. He pretended the kids at school wanted to be his friend instead of making fun of him, like they really did. And he pretended he was driving far away from Harmony without looking back.

Then he stopped pretending and had himself a good cry.

THIRTEEN

The next day, Walter and Posey sat on the porch steps with Porkchop and listened to Banjo complain.

"Anybody who thinks sleeping in the back of a truck is a good idea oughta be run out of town," he said, putting both hands on his back and shaking his head.

Then he leaned over the engine of his truck and muttered under his breath. Every now and then, he tapped on something with a wrench or jiggled a hose.

"Maybe it's the fuel pump," Posey said.

"Or the carburetor," Walter said. Tank's truck had always seemed to have a problem with the carburetor.

Banjo laid the wrench down on the fender of the truck and wiped his greasy hands on his overalls.

"Well, ain't I lucky my truck broke down right here in the midst of a couple of mechanical geniuses?" he said. Then he bowed slightly and made a dramatic sweep of his arm. "Step right on over here and be my guest, geniuses."

Just then Evalina came out onto the porch and said, "Mr. Fairweather, if I may be so bold as to make a suggestion—"

"Stop!" Banjo held up a hand. "Please, Miss Angel, call me Banjo. And you may be so bold as your heart desires."

"I was thinking it's probably time to call a mechanic," Evalina said.

"Why, Evalina," Banjo said. "I *am* a mechanic. Been working on engines since I was a mere boy. I could replace a fan belt before I could spit straight."

"Suit yourself," Evalina said and went back inside.

"Maybe you've lost your touch," Posey said.

Banjo's face turned red. "This truck is older than you are. I have oiled, polished, installed, and otherwise repaired every spark plug, gasket, and hose under this fair hood." He patted the hood lovingly. "I'll have this thing singing like a choirboy in no time."

"If that truck's so great," Posey said, "how come you want to win that key grab competition so bad?"

"A fine and fair question," Banjo said. "Trucks are like people. They don't live forever. When your number's up, it's up. This truck here has lived a long and fruitful life, but I fear her number is almost up. I must be prepared." He gave his truck another loving pat on the fender. "*That* is why I *will* win that new truck. Then this old vehicle can finally rest for all eternity in the junkyard of heaven."

And so the afternoon drifted by. While Banjo tinkered with the truck, Posey read to Walter from *Nuggets of Knowledge*.

"Hey, check out this nugget," she said. "The most words ever spoken by a parrot. Some dude swears he heard a parrot recite the entire Declaration of Independence. Can you believe that?"

She stabbed a finger onto a page.

"And get this," she said. "I bet you didn't know cows sweat."

Walter didn't really care that cows sweat. He couldn't get his mind off that tidy bedroom that used to be Tank's or those boxes piled up in the corner of the barn. That morning, he had stomped into the kitchen to ask his mother why she had done such a thing. But when he saw her droopy shoulders and those dark circles under her eyes while she sat forlornly at the kitchen table, he just couldn't bring himself to do it.

So he had gobbled down his cereal and hurried out of the house to watch Banjo work on his truck.

"Aha!" Banjo hollered suddenly, making Walter jump and Porkchop let out a loud yip. He threw both arms up and said, "Distributor cap."

"Is that bad?" Walter asked.

"No, son," Banjo said, "that is good. Cheap and easy to fix. So now I will rely on my considerable charm to convince the angelic Evalina to drive me to the auto parts store, after which I will fix this truck and continue on my bodacious adventure."

Walter jumped up. "Hey! I have an idea. Me and Posey can go, too, and Evalina can drop us off at the Chattahoochee bridge. It's easy to walk along the river from there so we can look for your hot-air balloon."

"Great idea," Banjo said.

Then he and Walter looked expectantly at Posey.

She nodded. "I agree. Good idea."

She turned to Banjo and said, "Go work your magic on No-Nonsense Evalina, Prince Charming."

Walter, Posey, and Porkchop jumped out of the back seat of Evalina's car and watched as she headed up the road toward town.

Banjo had been successful in using his considerable charm to convince Evalina to drive him to the auto parts store.

Walter had convinced her that he knew the way back home from the river.

And Posey had had the brilliant idea to bring her binoculars.

They walked along the path that ran beside the river, stopping every now and then so Posey could scan the water through the binoculars, but there was no sign of Banjo's *Starcatcher*. When the noonday sun began to beat down hot and heavy, Walter sat on the riverbank and wiped the back of his neck.

"I hope that balloon didn't sink in the river," he said.

Posey scooped up Porkchop and sat on the mossy ground beside Walter. "It didn't," she said.

"How do you know?"

Posey shrugged. "Just a feeling."

"What if the current carried it way on down yonder?" Walter nodded toward the river that snaked back and forth as far as they could see.

"We'll find it," Posey said.

Walter looked at Posey and couldn't help but admire how she always seemed so sure about things.

"Yeah," he said, trying to muster up his most confident voice. "We'll find it."

He sure hoped Posey was right. He had spent his whole life playing in the woods and exploring the riverbanks, but he had never found a hot-air balloon. He had also never seen one floating in the sky.

Wouldn't that be something?

Starcatcher drifting along up there among the clouds?

Posey stood up and gave Porkchop a kiss on the nose. "Let's go home," she said.

When they got to Walter's house, Posey went straight to the garden and turned on the hose. She took long gulps, letting the water splash mud onto her legs. Then she held the hose while Porkchop lapped at the water.

"What do you want to do now?" she asked.

Walter shrugged.

Suddenly Posey sat up and pointed to the barn. "Is that a hayloft up there?"

"Um, yeah."

Posey nodded toward a large oak tree beside the barn. "Let's make a rope swing in that tree! Then we can jump out of the hayloft on the swing."

Before Walter had a chance to even blink, Posey and Porkchop were racing toward the barn.

Before he had a chance to yell, *Wait!* Posey had yanked the barn door open.

Then when Posey said, "Whoa!" Walter knew it was too late.

Posey had seen Tank's truck.

FOURTEEN

By the time Walter got to the barn, Posey was walking around the truck.

She ran her hand along its shiny sides.

She stroked the gleaming silver hood ornament.

She traced the lightning bolt with a finger.

"Don't touch that!" Walter hollered.

Posey jerked her hand away from the truck and stared at him, wide-eyed. A rosy pink flush worked its way from her neck to her cheeks.

"Why not?" she said.

Walter yanked a towel out of the peach basket and began frantically rubbing the side of truck. The hood ornament. The lightning bolt.

His face burned.

His hands shook.

His chin quivered.

Do *not* cry, he told himself.

Instead of crying, he yelled.

"Who said you could come in here and touch this truck?"

Posey looked down at the dusty barn floor and said in a tiny, un-Posey-like voice, "Sorry."

Silence settled around them.

A shaft of sunlight from the window in the hayloft pierced the shadowy barn and danced on the hood of the shiny truck.

Walter could hear his own heart beating. Could feel the heat from his burning cheeks floating around him. He kept his eyes on the towel in his hand and said, "This is Tank's truck."

Posey shuffled her feet a little and said, "Oh."

Walter took a deep breath. "I mean, this *was* Tank's truck," he said.

"Oh."

For the first time ever, Walter said the words: "Tank died."

Posey said, "Oh," again, but then added, "Who's Tank?"

"My brother."

"Why's he called Tank?"

"'Cause he was big," Walter answered. "Built like a tank, everybody always said."

Then Walter told Posey about his brother.

That he had been so good at football and all the girls had loved him except Racine Reese, who got so mad at him one time that she threw a soda can at him and chipped his front tooth.

That he had taught Walter how to crack his knuckles and once made jelly-bean sandwiches for them to eat in their fort.

That he could do a backflip off the Chattahoochee bridge and broke his collarbone riding a skateboard down the courthouse steps.

That he had loved this truck more than anything and made Walter promise to take care of it when he joined the army.

And that he had gone to war overseas and was never coming home.

Walter slowly lifted his eyes and looked at Posey. Her face was pale, making her heart-shaped birthmark look darker. In a very soft voice, she said, "That's so sad."

Walter balled his fists and squeezed his eyes shut and told himself not to cry.

But he did.

He felt the tears running down his cheeks and his face burning with shame. Now Posey would probably think he was a baby and she would join those kids at school who didn't want to sit beside him in the cafeteria.

But then something unexpected happened. Posey put her hand on his arm and gave it a little pat.

Walter felt his heavy heart lift a little.

"Aren't you glad I moved here?" Posey said.

Yes, Walter *was* glad Posey had moved here. She had shown up in the middle of the night with her three-legged dog and her *Nuggets of Knowledge* and made him forget about how lonely he'd been. She didn't care about his pigeon toes or his lazy eye. And now here they were, the two of them, helping Banjo with his bodacious adventure.

Posey gave him a poke with her elbow. "I bet I can do a backflip off the Chattahoochee bridge," she said. She gave him another poke and added, "I bet you can, too."

Walter shrugged. "I doubt it."

"Oh, good grief," Posey said. "You gotta think

positive. That's rule number one in my second favorite book besides *Nuggets of Knowledge*. It's called *Caesar Romanoff's Rules for Making Friends*."

Walter stood up a little straighter. "Rules for making friends?"

Posey nodded.

Walter felt his heart lift even higher and his whole body seemed lighter.

"I could probably use that book," he told Posey.

"Oh, I know all the rules by heart. I'll teach 'em to you and you can practice with me."

"Okay."

So what had started out so bad with Posey touching Tank's truck and him crying right there in front of her had turned out pretty good with the promise of learning how to make some friends. Maybe even thwarting some bullies. Shoot, maybe even doing a backflip off the Chattahoochee bridge.

FIFTEEN

It had been nearly dark by the time Evalina and Banjo got back from town the day before, so Banjo had slept in the back of his truck again and planned to fix it the next day. Then he could drive along the river to look for the balloon. Walter had pushed aside his simmering feelings about Tank's room and begged and pleaded with his mama to let him go with Banjo. She kept saying Banjo seemed kind of wacky to her. But she finally agreed when Walter told her Evalina was letting Posey go.

When Walter got to Posey's that morning, Banjo was sitting on the porch, eating pancakes, and complaining to Posey.

"If I have to spend another night sleeping in that dang truck," he said, "this old back of mine is liable to lock up and y'all can just leave me for dead." He licked pancake syrup off his fingers. "Like this dern cast ain't enough to turn me into a hobbling fool." He scratched his arm. His neck. His leg. "And don't even say the word *mosquito*."

"Mosquito!" Posey hollered, and Walter couldn't help but laugh.

Evalina stepped out onto the porch and poured Banjo another cup of coffee. "Hopefully, you'll get your truck running today," she said.

"*Hopefully?*" Banjo said. "Why, Miss Evalina, you must trust me when I tell you that my truck will be purring like a kitten before the Georgia sun is straight up overhead and I am ready for my noontime nap."

Evalina smiled but Posey made a face. "Only babies take naps," she said.

"And old geezers like me," Banjo said. "Naps are the elixir of beauty. How you think I got so pretty? *Napping*, missy, napping."

Evalina roared with laughter. "Mr. Fairweather, you do have a way of brightening a day. I'll give you that," she said.

"Then my purpose in life has been achieved," Banjo said, giving his mustache a dramatic twirl. "I can now die a happy man."

* * *

All morning long, Walter and Posey played checkers while Banjo worked on the truck. Porkchop trotted around the yard, yipping at the chickens and sending the cats darting into the woods.

Just when Walter thought he couldn't stand one more game of checkers, Banjo called out, "Done! Fixed! Good as new!"

Walter and Posey let out a cheer and ran down to the truck.

"Can we go look for the balloon now?" Walter asked.

"Let's do it," Banjo said.

The three of them climbed into the truck and Porkchop hopped onto Posey's lap.

Banjo gave them a satisfied smirk when he turned the key and the engine started right up with a roar.

Walter's stomach churned with excitement. Now that they could drive along the river, surely they would find that hot-air balloon.

But when Banjo put the truck in gear, something bad happened.

Instead of going forward, the truck began to roll backward.

Banjo stomped on the brake with his good foot and the brake pedal went right down to the floor.

The truck kept rolling.

Banjo stomped on the brake again.

The truck kept rolling.

Slowly at first.

Then a little faster.

And a little faster.

Walter yelled, "Whoa!"

Posey hollered, "Stop!"

Porkchop barked.

Banjo let a string of cusswords fly.

And then, *bang.*

The rolling truck came to a sudden stop when it hit the large oak tree in the corner of Walter's yard.

Chickens squawked and scurried out of the way.

Cats leaped onto the porch.

Mama raced out the front door yelling, "What in tarnation?"

Banjo dropped his head back against the seat and said, "Well, if this ain't the icing on the cake of my hard-luck life."

SIXTEEN

While Banjo worked on the truck, Walter and Posey trudged through the woods, pushing aside low-hanging branches and stepping over moss-covered logs. Walter knew this way led to the river, but he had forgotten how dense and overgrown it was. Even Porkchop struggled to get around prickly shrubs and through tangled vines.

Walter swiped at the gnats swarming in front of his face. "Maybe this wasn't such a good idea," he said. "We probably should've stayed on the path."

Posey swiped at gnats, too. "But you said the river is just up ahead, right?"

"Right. But this is probably a waste of time. I don't see how we're ever going to find that balloon, especially with Banjo's truck broken down again."

Posey stopped and put her hands on her hips. "Walter Tipple!" she said. "Remember what I told you was rule number one in *Caesar Romanoff's Rules for Making Friends?*"

"I know, I know. Think positive," Walter said, "But this is gonna take forever."

They continued making their way through the dense woods, stepping over pricker bushes and swatting gnats. When they got to a small clearing, Posey sat in a patch of feathery ferns. "Let's take a break," she said. She pulled a floppy piece of cheese wrapped in plastic from her shirt pocket, unwrapped the cheese and tore it in half. "Want some?" she asked.

Walter shook his head.

Posey tore off a piece of cheese and tossed it to Porkchop, who caught it in midair.

"Sometimes I can't believe he only has three legs!" she said. "I wish I knew how he lost that leg. Evalina says he probably got it caught in a bear trap." She rolled some of the cheese into a ball and popped it into her mouth. Then she held up two fingers. "Now, here's rule number two for making friends," she said. "When you're talking to someone, always look 'em in the eye." She ducked her head toward Walter and stared into his eyes. "And say their name," she said. "Everybody *loves* to hear their own name."

"Okay."

"Let's practice. Tell me something and say my name."

"Um, well, um, nice weather we're having today, *Posey*."

Posey shook her head. "You left out one part of the rule."

"What part?"

"You gotta look me in the eye. Do it again."

Walter widened his eyes and stared straight into Posey's face. "Nice weather we're having, Posey," he said.

"That's better. Remember, look 'em in the eye and say their name."

She tossed another piece of cheese to Porkchop, then rolled the rest into a ball with her palms. "Okay, here's rule number three."

"I think we should keep going to the river," Walter said. "We're almost there."

"Look," Posey said. "If you want me to help you make friends, you gotta practice this stuff. Only a few more weeks till school starts."

Walter's stomach squeezed up at the thought of school. "Okay," he said.

"Rule number three is smile," Posey continued. "A lot. Now try it."

Walter felt silly but he smiled at Posey.

"No, not a little weeny smile!" Posey said. "A big, true smile. Like this."

She demonstrated a big, toothy grin.

Walter tried again, feeling even sillier.

"Perfect," Posey said. "Now let's combine rules two and three."

Walter sighed.

"Nice weather we're having today, Posey," he said, looking her in the eye and grinning.

"Very good."

Then she popped the ball of cheese into her mouth and said, "Let's go."

That night at supper, Walter stared glumly down at his plate. He poked his fork into the bright orange macaroni and cheese Mama had made from a box. She used to make the best homemade macaroni and cheese. It had been Tank's favorite.

But it didn't matter anyway because Walter didn't feel much like eating. He couldn't seem to get his niggling anger and pesky worries and swirling thoughts to settle down.

First, why had Mama cleared out Tank's bedroom? Did she expect Walter to just forget that his brother had ever lived here? He couldn't get rid of the lump in his throat every time he walked past that room. He wanted to open the door and see Tank's football trophies and the jumble of sheets on the bed and the blanket nailed over the window instead of the empty shelves and the perfectly made bed and the lacy curtains.

For another thing, school would be starting soon and no matter how many rules from Posey's book he learned, he wasn't convinced they would help him make friends. He could smile and call people by their names, but he'd still have that lazy eye and those pigeon toes. He'd still be puny and shy. And he'd never be like Tank.

Then there was that dream. The one about his birthday.

What did it mean?

But then, maybe it didn't mean anything.

His birthday was in just about two weeks. And even though Tank was there in that dream, in real life, he wouldn't be.

For the first time ever.

A birthday without Tank.

Walter stabbed at a piece of cold orange macaroni. At least his father would be home. He had called from somewhere in Texas and said there was no way he would miss Walter's birthday.

Deep down inside, a little seed of an idea was beginning to grow. What if he told Posey about his dream? She always seemed to have an answer for everything. Maybe she would know what his dream meant.

That night, Walter had the dream again. When he woke up, he sat on the side of the bed in his dark bedroom and, with the sweet smell of honeysuckle drifting through the open window, decided he would tell Posey about his dream.

SEVENTEEN

The next day, Walter sat out by the garden and listened to Banjo's angry mumbles drifting out of his truck. The part he needed to fix it had had to be ordered and no one seemed to know how long it would take. Banjo's friend Kudzu was supposed to be coming to take him home to Pine Mountain, but still hadn't shown up.

Posey was on the back porch, hunched over a piece of paper. She had drawn a map showing where the hot-air balloon started its flight from Pine Mountain, where Banjo had landed in the woods in Harmony, and several locations where the balloon might have come down by the Chattahoochee River. Her eyebrows squeezed together as she scribbled numbers.

"How fast did you say that balloon was going?" she called over to Banjo.

"I've told you three times," Banjo yelled from the truck. "By my calculations, which are most assuredly correct, I'd say six miles an hour."

Posey looked at Walter. "Okay, so I'm thinking that balloon probably landed about fifteen minutes after Banjo jumped." She did some more scribbling on her map. "So it must've gone about a mile and a half."

"But which direction?" Walter said.

She held up her map and pointed. "Probably this direction."

She walked over to Banjo's truck and gave it a pat. "Is this thing gonna be fixed today?" she asked.

"I am a lot of fine and noble things," Banjo said. "But I am *not* a magician."

"I thought you were the best mechanic in the world," Posey said.

Banjo swatted at flies hovering near his bad foot. He was no longer using crutches. Instead, he was hobbling around on the dirty blue cast. "Even the world's best mechanic can't rebuild a master cylinder in a day if they have to wait on the gol-dern parts."

He wiped the back of his neck with a handkerchief. Then he went on a tangent about the auto parts store.

"Hire a bunch of babies and that's what you get. Baby help, which is basically useless," Banjo grumbled. "That little ol' baby helper was a dang fool. His corn bread ain't cooked in the middle, I can tell you that."

Walter sighed.

It was clear that Banjo wasn't going to have his truck running today.

"Let's take your map down to the river," he called to Posey.

"Okay, here's Caesar Romanoff's rule number four," Posey said as she and Walter made their way toward the river, with Porkchop trotting along behind them. "Ask people lots of questions about themselves. Then when they tell you the answers, say things like 'Wow!' and 'No way!'" She pushed aside a thorny stem and held it for Walter. "That makes people feel special and they think you're interested in them. So, even if you're not, just fake it."

"Okay."

"Now try it," Posey said. "Pretend like you want to

be friends with me but we're just meeting for the first time."

"Um, well, um, good afternoon, *Posey*," Walter said, stopping to look Posey in the eye like he was supposed to from rule number two.

Posey nodded approvingly. "Very good!"

"Do you have any hobbies?" Walter asked.

"Why, yes, I do," Posey said. "I collect coins and I'm really good at Rubik's Cube." She smiled at Walter. "That's the truth, by the way."

"Um, oh, that's nice."

"No!" Posey said. "You're supposed to say 'Wow!' or 'No way!' to make me feel special."

"Oh, okay. Um, wow!"

"That was lame," Posey said. "Try again."

Walter's mind raced. Here was his chance. He was just going to go for it. "Have you ever had the same dream a bunch of times?" he asked.

Posey stopped and cocked her head. "You mean, like, a recurring dream?"

"Yeah."

"No. Have you?"

"Yes, I have."

"Really?"

Walter nodded.

"Wow!" Posey said. "And I'm not just saying that to make you feel special. What's the dream about?"

"Um, Tank," Walter said. All of a sudden he felt like he was going to cry. His chin began to quiver. He squeezed his eyes shut and concentrated on *not* crying. When he felt like he had things under control, he told Posey about the dream.

"How long have you been dreaming that?" she asked.

"Ever since Tank left."

"Wow," Posey said again. "And you never get to the part where you actually blow out the candles?"

Walter shook his head. "Never. I wake up at the same place every time."

"Hmmm." Posey scratched her chin. "When's your birthday?"

"August 5."

"Hmmm." Posey looked up at the sky. "I used to have a book about dreams but I had to take it back to the Goodwill when we left Tennessee." She looked at Walter. "Dang," she said. "I bet dreaming about your birthday and your dead brother means something, for sure."

Dead brother?

Those words stabbed Walter.

Deep and sharp.

Posey widened her eyes. "Oh, sorry!" she said.

"That's okay."

But Walter still felt the sting of those words.

"Maybe it means you're going to become just like Tank," Posey said. "You know, cool and confident."

"Ha!" Walter said. "That'll be the day."

"Or maybe you're going to win a trip around the world!" Posey said.

Walter shook his head. "Not very likely."

"Maybe Tank is a ghost and will come to visit you on your birthday."

Walter felt the blood drain from his face and his hands began to tremble at the thought of Tank being a ghost.

Posey shook her head. "Naw. That's crazy. That won't happen," she said.

"Maybe that dream doesn't mean anything," Walter said.

Posey clapped him on the back. "You know, one time I dreamed that I looked in the mirror and I looked like a movie star. Perfect skin and perfect hair like those girls in magazines. I even had a crown. But guess what happened when I woke up?"

"What?"

"I looked in the mirror and it was just me. Same ol' face. Same ol' hair. No crown, that's for sure."

Walter wasn't sure why Posey was telling him this.

"My *point*," she went on, "is that sometimes maybe dreams are supposed to make you feel good for just one little blip in your life. One little blip of feel-good you might be needing in your otherwise sorry existence."

Walter thought about that for a minute.

A blip of feel-good?

Maybe.

But then again, maybe not.

EIGHTEEN

Walter sat by his bedroom window and stared out at the starry summer sky. Banjo's snores drifted from the back of the broken-down truck, resting against the oak tree in the yard. His friend Kudzu still hadn't shown up like he was supposed to. Evalina said she would give him a ride back to Pine Mountain but Banjo had proclaimed himself far too much of a gentleman to take advantage of the goodness of an angel.

"Oh, my dear, dear Evalina," he had said. "I could never live another day with myself if I imposed upon you like that. All that dern construction over on Highway 14 has caused a detour that would inconvenience you far more than this gentleman could endure." He glanced over at his truck, resting against the oak tree in

Walter's yard. "I would walk over hot coals barefoot for you, so one more night under the stars means nary a thing to Jubilation T. Fairweather."

Posey, of course, kept saying, "Oh, brother."

Then Banjo had mumbled under his breath about what a lousy friend Kudzu was before climbing into the back of his truck for the night.

"Hurry up!" Posey called from out by the mailbox the next morning. "I got a good feeling about today!"

Walter gulped down the last of his orange juice and dashed out the door, letting the screen slam with a *bang* and making Mama holler something after him.

"I got a good feeling about today!" Posey said again. Her face was sunburned and freckled, that heart-shaped birthmark deep purple. She wore a *Save the Bees* T-shirt that came down to her knees. She turned and marched briskly toward the woods with Porkchop hop-trotting behind her.

"Hurry up!" she called over her shoulder.

Walter scurried after her, tossing the last piece of his toast to Porkchop. "Why are we going this way?" he asked.

Posey took a wrinkled piece of paper from the pocket of her shorts and unfolded it. She pointed to the map on the paper. "I'm thinking that the wind could've carried the balloon in this direction," she said.

Walter shook his head. "That doesn't seem right to me. Besides, if it landed in the river, the current would have carried it in *that* direction." He pointed in the opposite direction from where they were headed.

"Trust me," Posey said.

The path got narrower and narrower until it disappeared completely. Now they had to trudge through prickly holly bushes and weave around chokeberry trees and scraggly dogwoods.

Every now and then, Porkchop disappeared into the thick brush. Walter worried he might get lost and not come back but Posey didn't seem the least bit concerned. And, luckily, Porkchop always showed up again, his scruffy fur full of burrs.

Finally, Walter stopped. "This is crazy," he said. "It's too hot to be doing this."

Posey held up five fingers. "Rule number five according to Caesar Romanoff is quit your griping."

"Yeah, right."

"It is!"

Walter raised his eyebrows. "Quit your griping?"

"Well, not those exact words, but that's what he meant," Posey said. "No one wants to be friends with a griper."

"This doesn't seem like the best way to get to the river," Walter said.

"Okay, then, how would you get there. Helicopter?"

Walter shrugged.

"Then let's just keep going," Posey said. "It's not much farther."

Sure enough, after a few more minutes in the dense woods, they came to the river. The air was cooler and the gently flowing water made soft gurgling noises.

They continued on, following the bank of the river, until a most surprising and wondrous thing happened.

They rounded a bend and there, stuck in a cluster of pickerelweed and cattails, was Banjo's hot-air balloon.

NINETEEN

Walter and Posey stopped walking at the same time.

They said, "Whoa!" at the same time.

They scrambled down the bank to the river at the same time.

"That's it!" Walter hollered. "That's Banjo's balloon!"

Posey pumped her fist and let out a "Whoo-hoo" that echoed across the water. "*Starcatcher*!" she yelled.

Porkchop waded into the shallow water at the edge of the river, sniffing at the balloon and wagging his tail.

The silky fabric was exactly as Banjo had described it.

Every color of the rainbow with silver stars and golden moons.

But now it was torn and muddy, part of it swirling among the cattails and part of it under the murky water.

Beyond the weedy shallow water, attached to the fabric by cables, was a very large wicker basket, partially submerged in the deeper part of the river.

On top of the wicker basket was a metal frame. At the top of the frame were two round cylinders.

"Those are *burners*!" Posey said, pointing at the cylinders. "Wanna know how I know that?"

"How?"

"From my book *Land, Sea, and Air: A Child's Book About Transportation*," Posey said. "Evalina made me leave it in Tennessee. There was a chapter about hot-air balloons. The burners heat the air inside the balloon. *That's* what makes the balloon rise. You know why?"

"Why?"

"Because hot air rises."

Walter nodded. "Cool," he said. But he didn't want to get a science lesson from Posey. He wanted to get the balloon out of the river.

"Let's pull it out," he said.

He waded knee-deep into the water, his sneakers making sucking noises in the goopy mud as he walked. He grabbed some of the fabric and pulled. "It's heavy. Come help me."

"No way!" Posey said. "There's liable to be water moccasins in there."

Walter looked down at the water. Posey had a point. There definitely might be water moccasins. He had lived by the Chattahoochee River his whole life and had spent many summer days exploring the shallow waters or fishing along the riverbank. He had seen water moccasins a few times, slithering through the weeds or sunning on rotten logs.

He dropped the balloon fabric and hurried out of the river, sending water and mud flying and making Posey yell, "Hey, watch it!"

They stood on the riverbank and stared over at Banjo's Bodacious Adventure, now a sad, torn, and muddy mess.

"What do we do now?" Walter asked.

Posey shook her head. "I think Jubilation T. Fairweather is the only one who can answer that."

Walter nodded. "I guess you're right."

Banjo was napping in the back of his pickup truck when Walter and Posey raced out of the woods calling, "We found it!"

Banjo sat up with a jerk and clutched his heart. "Ain't you two got anything better to do than give me a heart attack?"

"We found *Starcatcher*!" Walter said, resting his hands on his knees and trying to catch his breath.

Banjo sat up and grabbed the side of the truck. "My balloon? My life? My heart? My bodacious adventure?" He looked up at the sky. "My prayers have been answered. This is a glorious day!"

Posey climbed onto the bumper of the truck. "Then I guess you've been praying that your balloon would be torn and muddy and halfway sunk into a river full of water moccasins," she said.

Banjo's grin dropped instantly. "Why you wanna rain on my parade?" he said. "You like watching a pitiful, one-legged man suffer?"

Posey shook her head. "No. Just preparing you for the truth is all. Right, Walter?"

Walter nodded but he felt bad for Banjo. He had gone from a look of sheer joy to one of total dejection in a blink.

Banjo wheezed and grunted as he struggled to climb out of the truck. Porkchop nipped at his ankle and made snarly noises. "Get this crazy mutt away from me," he said.

Posey motioned for Porkchop to come sit by her, which he did, although he still growled a little while keeping his eyes on Banjo.

"Well, what're we standing here for?" Banjo said. "We gotta go get my balloon. Two able-bodied young'uns ought to be able to get my precious *Starcatcher* out of the river under the guidance of yours truly, Mr. Jubilation T. Fairweather."

"Only a few things wrong with that suggestion," Posey said.

"Okay, Miss Rain Cloud," Banjo said. "What might those things be?"

"First of all," Posey said, "you will never make it through those woods with that cast on your foot."

Walter nodded in agreement. "Also, that balloon is very wet and very heavy," he said. "And that basket thing is filled with water and mud."

"Even if by some miracle we got it out of the water, then what?" Posey said. "No way can we carry that thing back here. Right, Walter?"

Walter gave Banjo a sympathetic look. "Right."

Banjo leaned dejectedly against the truck. "Of course she's right. But old Jubilation here will not be stopped by such minor obstacles. I *will* figure this conundrum out."

He closed his eyes and tapped his finger on his chin while Walter and Posey watched in silence.

Walter glanced up at the sky. Thick, dark clouds had begun to gather.

Uh-oh.

Walter suddenly had a thought that might add to Banjo's conundrum.

Should he share that thought with Banjo?

He took a deep breath and said, "There's something that has occurred to me that I think I should share."

Banjo and Posey both looked at him in surprise.

"Well?" Banjo said.

"If we get a heavy rain, the current in the river is liable to pick up enough to untangle that balloon from the weeds. If that happens, it might get carried off down the river or sink completely."

And then the craziest thing happened.

It began to rain.

TWENTY

It rained and rained and rained some more.

A torrential rain that clattered thunderously on the metal roof of the garden shed in Walter's yard and left the Queen Anne's lace by the mailbox bowing clear down to the ground.

Walter sat on Posey's covered porch and listened to Banjo telling Evalina some highly unlikely tales.

Like the time his aunt Becky chased the mailman with a tire iron for bringing her too many bills.

"Served two months in the county jail for that one," Banjo said. "I took her a bag of boiled peanuts every Sunday and when she died she left me $340 and a leaf blower."

Evalina laughed while Posey just doodled on her map.

Walter, however, was only half listening. He watched the rain forming giant puddles of muddy orange water out in the yard and thought about the river. The more it rained, the more he worried. He knew how much a rain like this could change the river.

The water would rise higher and higher, spilling onto the riverbanks and maybe even touching the bridges that passed over it.

The current would get faster and faster, forming eddies of frothy water that swept up small trees and washed the moss clean off boulders at the river's edge.

So it didn't really take a lot of imagination to picture the river churning around the cattails that held the balloon. It might swirl and swirl until it yanked the colorful fabric free.

Maybe the balloon was riding the current down the river at this very minute. Farther and farther away.

Or maybe the wicker basket attached to the fabric was taking on so much water that it was sinking.

The thought of either one of those scenarios weighed heavy on Walter. He had wanted so badly to rescue that balloon and one day see it floating above him in the Georgia sky. What a grand sight that would be!

But if it kept raining, that might not happen.

"One time at a truck stop in Waco, Texas," Banjo was telling Evalina, "I played poker for two days and two nights, living on beef jerky and warm beer. I won $438 and a riding lawn mower. I rode that lawn mower forty miles to the next town where I traded it for the very pickup truck that lies before you over there in Walter's yard."

"You mean the one that doesn't run?" Posey said.

"That's the one," Banjo said. "But soon as that part comes in, I will fix that truck like the master mechanic that I am and it *will* be running." He poked a finger at Posey. "I can guarantee you that."

Just then a very loud car came roaring up the road toward them, sending muddy rainwater shooting out in every direction. It stopped in front of Evalina's house and the driver honked the horn and rolled down the window.

Porkchop ran down to it, barking, until Posey called him back.

Banjo squinted through the pouring rain.

"Curtis?" he said. "Is that you? Where in blue blazes is Kudzu? I been trying to call him for three days."

"He got tied up over in Sandy Springs," Curtis said. "Asked me to come instead."

Banjo muttered a few grumbly words under his breath and made his way through the pouring rain toward the car.

"Never fear," he called over his shoulder. "I shall return."

That evening after dinner, Walter sat in Tank's truck and told his brother about Banjo and the hot-air balloon.

"Then me and Posey found that balloon and I wish you could've seen it," he said. "Silver stars and golden moons."

He sat back against the seat and listened to the rain on the roof of the barn. "I hope it's still there after this rain."

He got out of the truck, wiped the door handle with a towel, and whispered good night to Tank.

Then he went inside the house and climbed into bed. He said his prayers and closed his eyes and had that dream again.

TWENTY-ONE

Walter sat by the open window in the living room. The torrential rain had lasted more than two days, but had finally settled down to a soft drizzle. Outside, raindrops plunked from the tree branches into the muddy puddles in the yard and the air had that clean, rain-washed smell.

Banjo had called Evalina to say the part that he needed to fix his truck still wasn't at the auto parts store. In the meantime, that balloon was swirling around in the cattails at the edge of the Chattahoochee River.

Or was it?

Maybe it was drifting along the river on its way to Florida.

Or maybe it was resting in the mud way down on the dark, murky bottom of the river.

Walter sighed and pressed his face against the window screen. He thought about that day he had said good-bye to Tank at the bus station downtown. Tank kept hugging Mama and ruffling Walter's hair and looking at his reflection in the window. His uniform so clean and starched. Daddy gave him a couple of $20 bills and then Tank waved one last time, grinning like it was the happiest day of his life. After he climbed on that bus and disappeared, everything had been so quiet and empty and boring.

Until now.

Now there was Posey and Banjo and a hot-air balloon.

Who would've ever guessed that?

If only Tank were here.

Walter knew exactly how things would be.

Tank wouldn't need Posey telling him about *Caesar Romanoff's Rules for Making Friends*. Shoot, Tank could've written that book.

And if Tank had found Banjo's balloon, he wouldn't've cared one little bit if there were water moccasins in that river. He'd've jumped right on in there and pulled that balloon out all by himself.

If only Tank were here.

But he wasn't.

So Walter decided right then and there that he was going to do what Tank would've done. He was going to do everything in his power to get Banjo's balloon out of the river, and someday everyone in Harmony would look up in the sky and there it would be, floating lazily over the dirt roads and farms. The gas stations and diners. The post office and the auto parts store and the water tower with HARMONY painted on it in red.

When the rain finally stopped, Walter checked his backpack one more time. Some nylon rope. Garden clippers. His mother's old rusty loppers with wooden handles. Things they might need to get the balloon out of the river and secure it so it wouldn't get washed away by the current.

When he got outside, Posey was waiting by the mailbox wearing her dirty rain boots. Porkchop wandered around the yard, lapping up water from the puddles and making the chickens squawk.

"You brought that stuff we talked about, right?" Posey asked.

Walter nodded. "That's why this backpack weighs about a hundred pounds."

"I bet you don't know why *lb* is the abbreviation for the word *pound*," Posey said, leading the way toward the woods. She didn't wait for Walter to answer. "'Cause *lb* is short for *libra*, which is the Latin word for *pound*."

"*Nuggets of Knowledge*, right?" Walter asked.

"Yep."

As they made their way toward the river, Posey updated Walter on Banjo.

"I swear, he calls that auto parts store every five minutes and then calls Evalina to tell her those guys who work there are a bunch of baby imbeciles," she said. "And he's getting that guy Curtis to drop him off here today, supposedly so he can check on his truck but I think he just wants to see Evalina."

Eventually they came to two paths branching out in opposite directions.

"This way," Walter said, leading Posey and Porkchop farther into the woods until they finally came to the river. But when they got to the place where the balloon had been, they stopped.

The balloon was gone.

TWENTY-TWO

There was not even one little sign that the balloon had been there.

Not a broken cattail.

Not a piece of fabric with silver stars and golden moons.

Nothing.

Walter watched the water flowing swiftly along and let out a big heaving sigh. "Shoot," he said. "We're never going to find that balloon now."

Posey marched over and grabbed him by the shoulders.

"Don't you remember Caesar Romanoff's rule number one?"

"I know, I know," Walter said. "Think positive. Then I hope that balloon is floating down the river and not laying at the bottom of it."

Walter knew the Chattahoochee River flowed for miles and miles. That balloon could be way farther than he and Posey could walk, but he guessed it was worth a try.

They trudged along the rain-soaked riverbank while the hot Georgia sun beat down, making the air thick and steamy. Walter's backpack seemed to get heavier with every step.

As they walked, Posey jibber-jabbered like usual.

"When we lived in Tennessee, Evalina decided to have a day care right there in our living room. Talk about a bad idea!"

"How come?"

"You ever heard a room full of babies crying all day? And Evalina's never exactly been the Princess of Patience. She'd change diapers and mash up bananas but those babies wouldn't *never* hush up." She pushed a strand of sweaty hair out of her eyes. "I figured maybe they took one look at my ugly mug and all the bananas in the world wouldn't make them stop their squalling."

Walter wondered if his lazy eye would make babies cry.

"One time Ernest and Nadine, you know, those

grandparents I never met?" Posey went on. "They sent me a whole box of clothes. *Whoo-ee*. You should've heard Evalina going on and on about how her parents never did nothing for her and now here was a box of charity. She taped that box up and scribbled *Return to Sender* on it. Then she made a beeline to the post office and sent it right back."

Suddenly Walter stopped.

"Look!" He pointed toward the river ahead of them.

Posey's mouth dropped open. Then she let out a whoop.

They raced along the edge of the water, Walter's backpack thunking heavily against his back, Posey's rain boots clomping on the hard-packed clay of the river-bank, and Porkchop running in that hopping way of his.

When they stopped, Walter and Posey grinned at each other and high-fived.

There, in front of them, was the balloon, torn and muddy, floating in the shallow part of the river. The wicker basket attached to it was wedged against a cypress tree that leaned over the water.

Walter's heart raced as he examined the balloon. He felt like he'd been waiting his whole life for an adventure like this to come along and now it had. He looked up at the sky and imagined that balloon drifting by, floating over the river and gliding through the clouds.

Suddenly Posey interrupted his happy daydream.

"Okay, so now we have to get it out," she said.

"Right." Walter waded into the murky water and tugged on the balloon, determined not to think about water moccasins. To be brave like Tank would've been. Porkchop trotted back and forth on the riverbank, barking.

"It's not tangled up like last time," Walter said. "I think we can do it."

"What about water moccasins?" Posey said.

"Don't worry about it," Walter said. "You've got boots on."

He looked down at his bare legs and soaked sneakers standing in that water and a little niggle of fear began to tap at him. But he closed his eyes briefly and pictured Tank. Heard him say, *You got this, little man.*

"I don't know," Posey said. "What if a water moccasin swims right down inside my boot?"

Then Walter did a very un-Walter-like thing. He waded farther into the water and said to Posey, "Remember Caesar Romanoff's rules about thinking positive and quit your griping. Help me pull this thing out."

A flicker of surprise flashed across Posey's face, but she grabbed the edges of the balloon and began to pull.

The soaked fabric was heavier than Walter had imagined it would be.

He and Posey tugged and tugged.

Before long, they were both soaked and muddy and out of breath, but the balloon was finally completely out of the water.

"Okay, now we tie the basket to that tree so it can't get washed away again," Walter said.

He took the nylon rope out of his backpack and he and Posey worked together to secure the wicker basket to the tree. Then they rolled up the colorful fabric and tied it to smaller trees and shrubs along the riverbank.

When they were done, Posey glanced at the bridge over the river just ahead. "What if somebody sees it?" she said. "People driving over that bridge might see it."

As usual, Posey was right. The balloon *would* be easy to see from the bridge. And if someone saw it, they might come down here and take it.

"I have an idea," Walter said. "Let's cut a bunch of branches and lay them over the balloon to camouflage it."

So that's what they did. Used the loppers and

clippers from Walter's backpack to cut sprigs of gray-beard shrubs, chokeberry, and wild dogwood and laid them over the balloon until it was almost completely covered.

Finally they stepped back and examined their work.

"Perfect," Posey said.

"Perfect," Walter said.

"Now what?"

"Now as soon as Banjo's truck is fixed, he can come get his balloon," Walter said.

Posey looked around her at the scrub bushes and clusters of trees. "How's he supposed to get a truck down here?"

Walter grinned and wiggled his eyebrows. "I happen to know where there's a logging road that comes right to the riverbank up yonder near the bridge."

"What's a logging road?" Posey asked.

"My daddy told me how the logging company used to take logs down to the river so they could put them on boats. They cut roads all through these woods. I bet I know every single one of them."

Posey gave Walter a slap on the back and said, "Perfect."

TWENTY-THREE

Walter and Posey burst out of the woods, followed by Porkchop, who was yipping joyfully. Banjo was sitting on the bumper of his truck, cleaning his fingernails with a pocketknife.

"Banjo!" Posey called.

"Sweet jumping Jupiter," Banjo said, clutching his heart. "You 'bout made me cut my finger plumb off, missy."

"Did you fix your truck?" Walter asked.

Banjo frowned. "Still waiting on the part I need," he said. "But I had Curtis bring me back to check on things."

"Well, guess what?" Posey said. "*Starcatcher* was washed away by the rain."

Banjo's face fell.

"But we found it again!" Walter said. "So we tied it up and camouflaged it so nobody will see it."

"Well, I'll be doggone!" Banjo's eyes twinkled and his twirly mustache lifted with his grin. "I ought to hang my head in shame to admit that I didn't have much faith in you two rescuing my beloved balloon. But instead, I'm going to shake your hands and demonstrate my overwhelming glee."

He hobbled over to Walter and Posey and shook their hands. Then he did a funny-looking jig right there in Walter's yard, sending the chickens scurrying and making Porkchop bark and snarl.

"Y'all have lifted me from the depths of despair right up to the very pinnacle of everlasting joy," he said. "You have showered me with blessings the likes of which I most definitely do not deserve."

"You need to get that balloon soon as you can," Walter said. "We did a pretty good job of covering it up, but still, somebody might find it if it stays there much longer."

"What if somebody takes it?" Posey asked.

"Don't say them words!" Banjo snapped. "There ain't nobody in this county wants to mess with Jubilation T.

Fairweather. But I ain't gonna worry about it. You wanna know why?"

"Why?" Walter and Posey said together.

"'Cause most of the stuff people worry about ain't never gonna happen anyway. Now leave me be while I climb in the back of this truck and get some beauty rest."

He climbed into his truck, fluffed up a couple of the old blankets back there, and in a blink, was snoring.

That evening at the supper table, Walter picked at his tuna casserole and tried to decide if he should tell his mom about finding Banjo's balloon. What if she didn't like him going so far down the river? What if she complained about Banjo being a nut, like she sometimes did?

But he decided to tell her. Maybe it would cheer her up.

He told her about how the balloon had been stuck in the cattails and then got carried away after the rain. He told her about how he and Posey found it again and tied it to a tree and camouflaged it so nobody could see it from the bridge.

"Wait'll you see it," he said. "It's exactly the way Banjo described it. Every color of the rainbow with silver stars and golden moons. It's ripped a little and kind of muddy, but I'm sure Banjo can fix it. The balloon is named *Starcatcher*."

His mother put her fork down and blinked at Walter like she had just noticed he was there.

"*Starcatcher*?" she said.

"Yes, ma'am."

She leaned toward Walter. "You know, I guess I was thinking Banjo is so, um, *eccentric*, that that whole hot-air balloon story was liable to be a bunch of baloney."

"No, it's true!" Walter said.

It had been so long since he and his mother had talked like this that once he got started, he could hardly stop, while the anger he had had about Tank's bedroom seemed to drift away.

He told his mother about the Macon County Key Grab and how Banjo was going to win a new truck.

"And just think about it, Mama," he said. "Imagine *Starcatcher* floating along in the sky with a bunch of other balloons."

Mrs. Tipple looked out the window and smiled.

A real smile.

Like she used to.

"That sounds real nice, Walter," she said.

She reached across the table and patted his hand.

Just the kind of pat he'd been needing.

After supper, Walter headed next door. Porkchop hop-trotted over to greet him with a yip.

"He's telling whoppers again," Posey said, jerking a thumb toward Banjo, who was sitting on the porch swing beside Evalina.

Walter smiled. Banjo *was* pretty good at telling whoppers.

Like how his cousin Big Ed lost fifty pounds by eating nothing but pork rinds and beets for six months.

How when Banjo was ten, he ate a live garter snake 'cause his brother Caleb offered him $3 to do it.

And that his granddaddy invented the Hula-Hoop.

Now he was telling Evalina about the time he tried to shoot a squirrel with a BB gun.

"That BB ricocheted off a telephone pole and hit the left front tire of a big black limousine coming down the highway." He leaned closer to Evalina. "And I can assure you that I like to died when the back door of that limo opened and who should step out but Dolly Parton!"

"No way!" Evalina said.

Banjo held up a hand. "May the good Lord strike me dead if that ain't the truth."

"Yeah, right," Posey said.

"Why you think I got this tattoo?" Banjo rolled up the sleeve of his shirt to show them the tattoo on his skinny arm. A big red heart with Dolly Parton's face smack-dab in the middle of it.

Evalina laughed and Walter said, "Wow!" But Posey seemed determined to stay unimpressed.

"Evalina," Posey said. "Tell Banjo about that time we went to Dollywood and you got sick on that tiny roller coaster."

Evalina blushed. "Posey," she said. "I don't think he wants to hear that."

"Wait here," Posey said. She jumped up and ran inside the house and came back with a shoebox full of photographs. She riffled through them, then held one up.

"Here we are in Pigeon Forge," she said.

Banjo took the photo from her. "Well, would you look at that?" he said. "Y'all could be sisters."

Evalina smiled. "Hardly," she said.

"And check this out." Posey held up another photograph. "This is me and Evalina building a little wooden car for the Pinewood Derby." She looked over at Evalina. "Remember that?"

"I sure do."

"And get this," Posey continued. "When we showed up at the Elks Club to race my car, they told us girls couldn't enter. But ol' Evalina here just put 'em in their place, right, Evalina?"

Evalina nodded.

"And guess what?" Posey said. "I came in second place."

"Now *that*," Banjo said, "is a story of true grit and fortitude."

Posey grinned. "True grit and fortitude," she said. "That's me and Evalina in a nutshell."

Before long the lightning bugs began to twinkle out in the yard, and Curtis's car came chugging up the gravel road.

Banjo said good night with a dramatic bow and climbed in.

Walter watched the car disappear from sight, then said good night and headed for home.

TWENTY-FOUR

The next morning, Walter dashed outside while the dew was still on the grass and the chickens were just beginning to stir. It was almost August and the Georgia heat settled still and heavy in the air by the time the sun was barely up. Not even a hint of a breeze. The garden was beginning to look tired. The zucchini grew large and fat on yellowing vines. The pole beans drooped lazily from a lattice made of string. The few heads of lettuce still left had long since gone to seed, sending up shoots of tiny white flowers.

Walter was surprised to see Banjo leaning over the open hood of his truck.

"Hey, Banjo," he said.

Banjo stood up straight and wiped his hands on a greasy towel. "Hey, there, young man."

"Whatcha doing?"

"Oh, just checking spark plugs and such so that when I finally get that gol-dern master cylinder rebuilt, she'll be in tip-top shape to fetch my beloved *Starcatcher*."

Walter smiled. He was pretty sure Banjo had come back to see Evalina.

Just then Posey ran out of her house and down the steps, with Porkchop hop-trotting along beside her. "Hey, y'all!" she called. She handed a grocery bag to Banjo, who was now sitting on the edge of the truck bed. "Evalina said you can have these tomatoes."

"Evalina. Evalina," Banjo said dreamily. He took the bag from Posey and closed his eyes. "Just the sound of that glorious name is like heavenly music wafting in this pure, sweet Georgia air that I breathe." He took a big, dramatic breath.

"Oh, brother," Posey said. Then she climbed up onto the back of the truck to sit beside Banjo. "When did Americans first eat tomatoes?"

"I'm sure you'll enlighten us," Banjo said, winking at Walter.

"Well, an Italian painter brought them to Salem, Massachusetts, in 1802, but people thought they were poisonous and wouldn't eat them." She scratched at mosquito bites on her legs. "It was almost another forty years before folks figured out they could eat them." She leaned toward Banjo. "That's from *Nuggets of Knowledge*. The French called them *love apples*. So weird, huh?"

"Love apples," Banjo whispered. He took a tomato out of the bag and bit into it, sending juice running down his chin. "That dear, dear Evalina is giving me a glimmer of hope. A token of her affection. A sly, sly symbol of the very depth of her heart." He looked at Posey. "Wouldn't you agree?"

Posey jumped off the side of the truck and landed with a *thud*. "Sorry to burst your bubble, Jubilation, but I would not."

Banjo climbed down from the truck, grunting and wheezing, and tossed a piece of tomato to Porkchop, who gobbled it up.

He poked a finger at Posey. "Why you wanna rain on my love parade? Now if y'all will excuse me, I'm going inside to call the auto parts store."

Then he clomped across the yard toward Posey's.

When he was gone, Walter turned to Posey and

asked, "Think we'll get that balloon before something happens to it?"

Posey shrugged. "I guess. But something tells me that Banjo isn't exactly Mr. Lucky."

Walter was going to remind Posey about Caesar Romanoff's rule number one, think positive, but then a string of angry words came roaring through the screen door of Posey's house.

"Uh-oh," Walter said.

"See what I mean?" Posey said.

Banjo came hobbling across the yard, kicking at gravel with his good foot and punching the air with his fists. Then he went on a rather long and curse-filled tirade about the auto parts store and those brainless babies who worked there.

When he finally stopped, Walter said, "So, I guess the truck part didn't come."

Banjo glared around the yard. "Hold me back, young man, for I am liable to choke a chicken with my bare hands."

Walter grabbed the back of Banjo's overalls, and Posey said, "Oh, good grief, calm down."

Banjo's face was still red and he was huffing and

puffing, but he leaned back against the truck and muttered under his breath about his dern bad luck.

"What about *Starcatcher*?" Walter asked.

"Without a truck, I am helpless to rescue my beloved balloon to fulfill my dream of a bodacious adventure," Banjo said. "Helpless, I tell you."

Posey nodded. "Helpless."

Walter looked wide-eyed from Banjo to Posey and back to Banjo again.

"So, you're just going to sit here and do nothing while someone might be taking that balloon this very minute?" he said.

"What else can I do?" Banjo said. "Here lies my good-for-nothing truck, unable to move. Without a truck, I fear I cannot rescue my beloved *Starcatcher*."

And then something very surprising happened.

Walter said something he had never expected to say.

Never in a million years.

The words just slipped out without the slightest hesitation.

"I have a truck," he said.

TWENTY-FIVE

Posey stared at Walter, her mouth open in surprise.

Banjo looked confused.

Walter stood there in disbelief.

Had he really said those words?

I have a truck.

Yes, he had said them.

The words danced around in his head.

Then two more words worked their way into his head.

The two words were *never* and *mind*.

He should say *Never mind*.

But he didn't have a chance because Posey was already skipping in circles and saying, "Yes! Now we're talking!"

And Banjo was saying, "Well, I'll be derned, boy. Why didn't you say something before now? Our problem is solved!"

Walter glanced over at the barn. "But nobody can drive it but me," he mumbled.

Posey and Banjo grew quiet.

Walter's mind raced.

What in the world was he thinking?

He couldn't drive that truck.

Could he?

Sure, he had cruised around in plowed-up bean fields with Tank beside him, but this was different.

He wouldn't take that truck down to the river.

Would he?

What if he scratched it?

Or worse?

And what about Mama? There was no way she'd let him drive Tank's truck.

Posey tapped her chin and looked up at the sky. "We need a plan," she said.

"A plan?" Banjo said. "Oh, for criminey's sake. What's there to plan? We drive the truck to the river and load up *Starcatcher*. Over and done."

"Slow down, Jubilation," Posey said. "Tell him about the truck, Walter."

Walter looked down at the patchy grass under his feet.

Over at the chickens, strutting around the yard.

At a couple of cats, sunning on the porch with twitching tails.

Then he sat down, stared at his sneakers, and told Banjo about Tank.

How he was captain of the high school football team and spent two years in the eighth grade.

How he taught Walter how to spit from the porch into a pickle jar.

How he once drove a motorbike right through the front doors of church.

How he won a hot-dog-eating contest three years in a row and sometimes skipped school.

"One time," Walter said, "me and Tank went way out County Road 19 and then down a bunch of dirt roads till we got to a plowed-up bean field." Walter couldn't help but smile at the memory. "Tank drove out slap-dab into the middle of the field and let me drive. He taught me how to speed up and then yank the steering wheel to make his truck spin around and around. Red dust and pebbles were flying out every which way and you should've heard Tank whooping it up."

Walter would never forget that feeling.

The two of them swallowed up in a cloud of dust, leaving tire tracks in giant circles all over that field.

Then Walter had to tell Banjo the hard part.

How Tank had joined the army and was never coming back.

And how he, Walter Tipple, had promised to take care of his truck.

"I'm taking real good care of it," Walter said. "So that's why nobody can drive it but me."

Banjo plopped down on the ground beside him with a grunt. "I haven't had many true disappointments in my life, but, son," he said. "I am truly disappointed that I never got to meet that brother of yours."

Walter nodded, his chin quivering.

Banjo slapped him on the knee and added, "I always did admire a man who could spit into a pickle jar."

Walter's chin stopped quivering and he smiled.

A little smile.

But still, a smile.

Then Posey piped up and said, "Now, let's talk about our obstacles."

Banjo looked up at her. "Obstacles? And what might those be?"

Posey sat down facing Banjo and Walter and rattled off the obstacles.

Evalina and Walter's mother, for one.

A ten-year-old boy driving a truck, for another.

Actually getting the truck to the riverbank where the balloon was, for another.

When she was finished, Banjo leaned forward and said, "Let me give you some advice, missy. Life is simpler when you plow around the stumps."

"What's that supposed to mean?"

"Means them so-called obstacles of yours are merely stumps." He clapped Walter on the back and said, "And we shall plow around them."

While Porkchop barked at cats in the garden, Walter, Posey, and Banjo sat in the back of Banjo's truck playing cards.

Well, not really playing cards.

Pretending to play cards.

That had been Posey's idea.

"Okay, so we've got to figure out how to plow around those so-called stumps," she had said, giving Banjo one of her famous eye rolls. "And if we just sit out here talking, it will look suspicious. I'll be right back."

She had run home and come back with a deck of cards.

So now they were pretend-playing and talking about how to plow around the stumps.

"The way I see it," Posey said, "the biggest stump, well, actually, the biggest *two* stumps, are Evalina and Mrs. Tipple. There's no way they're going to let us take that truck to the river. *Especially* with Walter driving."

Walter nodded. "Agreed."

Banjo nodded. "Agreed."

"But I, of course, have a brilliant idea," Posey said.

Walter and Banjo leaned forward, holding their cards.

Posey went on. "I happened to use my stealthy eaves-dropping skills to learn two vital pieces of information."

"And?" Walter said.

"And . . ." Posey held up a finger. "Number one: Evalina thinks your mama needs to have a hobby to take her mind off Tank." Then she blushed a little and hurriedly added, "Sorry."

Walter nodded. "That's okay."

"And she has convinced your mama to let her teach her how to quilt," Posey said. "Evalina is an award-winning quilter. She has blue ribbons from the county fair in Tennessee."

"To toss some words back to you that you so glee-fully toss to me," Banjo said, "will you get to the point?"

Posey whipped a folded-up postcard from her pocket. "*This* came in the mail this morning." She held the post-card for Walter and Banjo to see.

Fabric Sale
Up to 50% Off
One Day Only
Gail's Fabrics Galore

Banjo grinned. "Perfect! They'll wanna go there, for sure." He slapped his cards down in front of him and hollered, "Rummy!"

Walter tossed his cards down, too. "I don't know," he said. "Do you really think we can get them to go in to town today?"

Posey shook her head. "Not today." She pointed to a

135

date on the postcard. "The sale is tomorrow. I will have Evalina so excited about taking your mama to buy fabric that she will be jibber-jabbering about it all night."

"But still," Walter said. "Mama never wants to go anywhere anymore. I doubt if she'll go."

Banjo sat back and looped his thumbs through the straps of his overalls and shook his head slowly. "Young Walter Tipple," he said. "Have you forgotten that I, Jubilation T. Fairweather, possess the charm of a gallant prince, the smooth tongue of a poet, and the uncanny ability to convince a snake that it has legs?"

He gathered up all the cards and began to shuffle. As he was dealing a hand to each of them for another pretend game, he looked up through his bushy eyebrows and said with a smile, "Your mama *will* be going to town with Evalina tomorrow. Trust me."

Walter and Posey looked at each other and high-fived.

They had plowed around that stump.

But what about the others?

TWENTY-SIX

"Okay," Posey said. "That's settled. Now what about the other problems?" She glanced at Banjo. "I mean, stumps."

"Um, what are those?" Walter asked.

"Okay, we'll start with the obvious," Posey said. "Do you know how to drive that truck?"

Walter tried to look cool and confident when he said yes, but he had a feeling that he probably didn't.

Banjo poked him in the arm. "If you are to have us believe that you are an honorable man, then you must abide by the laws of honorable men," he said.

"What laws?"

"Oh, there are many," Banjo said. "But one of them is this: When an honorable man says yes, an honorable man means yes." He leaned toward Walter. "Are you an honorable man?"

"Um, sure." Walter was sorry to feel his face heat up with a blush that must have made him look less than honorable.

But he *did* know how to drive Tank's truck.

Hadn't he done it a bunch of times?

Or at least three or four times?

What was so hard about it, anyway? You push on the gas to go and step on the brake to stop, right?

"How are we going to plow around *this* stump," Posey said. "A ten-year-old kid driving on the highway? Everybody in Harmony'll be calling the cops." She shook her head. "Sorry. Bad idea."

Walter almost pointed out to her that he was practically eleven, but he decided to get right to the nitty-gritty.

"I know how to get to the river without driving on the main roads," he said.

Banjo lifted his eyebrows.

"The logging roads," Walter said.

"Oh yeah!" Posey said. "Tell Banjo about the logging roads."

"They're all through these woods," Walter said. "My

138

daddy's taken me on a bunch of them. Some of them are kind of overgrown with weeds and stuff, but I bet you can still drive on them." He leaned forward and whispered. "I know there's a road that leads to the Chattahoochee bridge close to where *Starcatcher* is." He paused for a little dramatic effect. "I'm pretty sure we can get close enough to get that balloon into the truck."

"But how will you get the truck from the barn to the logging roads?" Posey asked.

"*That*," Walter said, "is the easiest stump to plow around." He glanced behind him to make sure they were alone. "When I was little, before my daddy started driving a truck, he worked in the sawmill way up yonder on the other side of the river. My daddy and some of his friends made a clearing through the woods behind the barn so he could get to the logging roads without having to go all the way to the highway to get to work and back."

Banjo slapped his knee and laughed a wheezy laugh. "Well, if that ain't about the best news I ever heard, I don't know what is. Walter, you are a brilliant and honorable man."

The three of them looked proudly at one another. They had done it! They had plowed around the stumps.

Suddenly, out of nowhere, another stump jabbed at Walter and wiped that proud look right off his face.

"Uh-oh," he said.

Posey and Banjo waited.

"When we get *Starcatcher* in the truck, what do we do then?" Walter said. "We can't bring that balloon back here or else Mama and Evalina will know what we did." His stomach balled up in a knot of disappointment. Their plan wouldn't work.

Banjo tossed his cards down with a flourish and said, "Allow me to contribute my own stroke of genius to this most worthy and devious plan."

Walter leaned forward and Posey lifted her eyebrows.

"I happen to know that one can get from the Chattahoochee bridge practically to my back door without driving on the highway," Banjo said. "Right where the bridge ends, one can leave the highway by taking a sharp left into a very large field. If one drives a quarter of a mile across that field, one crosses the border into Pine Mountain. And if one continues approximately a quarter of a mile more, one will be on the property of the honorable Jubilation T. Fairweather." He grinned at Walter and Posey.

"How do you know there's not fences or cows or something in that field?" Posey asked.

"Because I am not ashamed to admit that I may have had a night or two of foolish revelry which necessitated a shortcut home." He leaned forward and whispered: "I may have used a little sleight of hand in a poker game or two that seemed to create some ill feelings in a few unsavory half-wits who took it upon themselves to try to follow me home for reasons I never cared to find out. So a shortcut through that field has come in mighty handy for ol' Banjo once or twice."

"You really think I could drive from the bridge to your property?" Walter asked.

"You can take my word for it, Mr. Tipple. And the word of Jubilation T. Fairweather is as good as gold."

Suddenly a car roared up the road and stopped beside them, with the window rolled down.

"Curtis?" Banjo said. "Don't tell me. Kudzu's got a board meeting with his stockholders today. Or maybe he needs to take his yacht down to Miami for the weekend."

Then he climbed out of the truck, muttering about his so-called friend Kudzu, got into Curtis's car, and waved goodbye.

Walter leaned back against the side of Banjo's truck and smiled.

They had plowed around every stump.

Walter should've been feeling good about their plan, but a little flutter of doubt hovered over him.

Could he really do this?

That night, Walter had the dream.

Same people.

Same cake.

Same everything.

Like always, he took a deep breath to blow out the candles and then woke up.

He lay there in the dark, blinking up at the ceiling. A sliver of moonlight cast a soft glow across his bedroom.

Walter tiptoed over to the window and looked up at the summer night sky.

The twinkling stars.

The occasional glow of heat lightning in the distance.

The sound of crickets echoed across the yard.

Walter closed his eyes and pictured his brother, Tank, grinning that chip-toothed grin of his.

And then the strangest thing happened.

He heard Tank's voice plain as day.

"I'll show you my world."

Walter's eyes flew open and he spun around, expecting Tank to be standing there in his fake leather jacket.

But of course Tank was not standing there.

Walter had only imagined it.

He also imagined Tank poking him in the arm and saying, "You got this, little man. You can do it."

"Really?" Walter whispered into the dark room.

He could swear he heard Tank say, "Sure! Do it!"

Walter felt a sudden rush of calm settle over him and could practically see his worries drift right out the window and disappear into the starry sky.

He *could* do this.

He could drive Tank's truck to the river to get *Starcatcher*.

By golly, tomorrow he *would*.

TWENTY-SEVEN

"Yoo-hoo!"

Walter looked up from the porch steps to see Evalina hurrying across her yard toward the garden, where Mama was picking squash. Right behind her came Posey and Porkchop.

"*This* is the quilt pattern we should make first," Evalina said, holding up a quilt with triangles of fabrics in colorful patterns.

"That's pretty, Evalina," Mrs. Tipple said. "But I don't know. I've never been much of a seamstress."

"Seamstress?" Evalina flapped a hand. "I'm telling you, this pattern is easy peasy. And guess what else?"

"What?"

Evalina whipped a postcard out of the pocket of her apron and said, "Gail's Fabrics Galore! Half-off sale! You can't beat that. Let's go into town and I'll help you pick out fabric."

Mrs. Tipple looked at the quilt. "I don't know," she said. "I'm not sure I'm up for that."

"It'll be good for you," Evalina said. "We can—"

Suddenly Porkchop raced toward the road, barking like crazy.

Who should be hobbling toward them but one very red-faced Banjo.

"Kudzu couldn't be bothered to drive me up here from the highway," he said.

Porkchop snapped at the air around Banjo. "Will you get that crazy mutt of yours away from me?" he said to Posey.

Posey ran over and put a hand on Porkchop's head. "Quiet, boy. He may look scary, but he's okay," she said.

Suddenly Banjo's face changed from red and angry to starry-eyed admiration.

"Why, Evalina," he said. "Do *not* tell me you made that exquisite quilt!"

Evalina blushed. "Why, yes, actually, I did."

Banjo held out both arms and let them drop with a slap against his sides. Then he turned to Posey and said, "Is there *nothing* that mother of yours can't do?"

Posey opened her mouth to answer but Banjo held up a hand. "Stop!" he said. "You don't even need to answer that."

He turned to Evalina and said, "Anyone who can make a quilt as glorious as that one already has a spot in heaven reserved just for them. Why, quilts such as that would keep the angels warm at night."

"Oh, good grief," Posey said.

Evalina chuckled. "You do have a way with words, Mr. Banjo." She motioned toward Mrs. Tipple. "I've been trying to convince Cora here to go into town with me so we can buy fabric for *her* to make a quilt like this."

Banjo hobbled over to the garden.

"Why, Mrs. Tipple, I have no doubt that you, too, could produce a quilt every bit as fine as this one," he said.

"Well, I don't know," Mrs. Tipple said. "I'm not very good at—"

"Mrs. Tipple!" Banjo interrupted. "You can do anything you set your mind to. I mean, look at that garden that's been providing an abundance of nourishment to your blessed family." He paused to fling an arm out toward the chicken coop. "Look at those lucky chickens who appear to be about the most contented chickens I've ever seen." He lowered his head and looked up through his bushy eyebrows. "And I have seen a lot of chickens in my day."

He slapped Walter on the back and said, "And anyone who can raise a fine young man such as this can surely make a quilt as lovely as that one."

Posey made a *pfft* sound and said, "I don't get the connection between raising a kid and making a quilt."

Banjo shot her a look that said, *Be quiet and let me handle this.*

Mrs. Tipple glanced up at the sky. "I don't know," she said. "It looks like it might rain. I'm not much in the mood to go into town, especially if it's raining."

"Oh, Cora, don't be silly," Evalina said. "We won't be long. I'll help you pick out fabric. It'll be fun."

Mrs. Tipple looked over at Walter. "I don't like leaving Walter alone and—"

"Never fear!" Banjo blurted. "If Theodore wasn't my middle name, Responsible would be. As well as Dependable and Practical and Quick-Witted. You two

147

fair ladies could not possibly leave your offspring in more capable hands."

Evalina looked at Mrs. Tipple and raised her eyebrows. "They'll be fine, Cora." Then she turned to Banjo. "Maybe you could fix those rotten porch railings like you said you would."

Banjo twirled his mustache. "I can fix anything your heart desires."

Mrs. Tipple pointed a finger at Walter. "You are to stay put," she said. "Don't go up there near the highway and don't go traipsing through the woods."

Walter nodded solemnly and tried hard to keep the look of guilt off his face. He never had been very good at disobeying grown-ups.

But actually, he *wasn't* going to go up there near the highway.

And he *wasn't* really traipsing through the woods.

Right?

He concentrated on trying to look normal instead of overflowing with guilt and excitement as Evalina and his mother got their purses and climbed into Evalina's car.

Walter, Posey, and Banjo stood motionless as the sound of Evalina's car grew fainter and fainter.

148

Then Banjo's loud whoop cut through the silence and Posey skipped gleefully in circles with Porkchop nipping playfully at her heels.

"Come on, y'all!" she hollered. "Let's go get *Starcatcher*!"

The three of them headed for the barn. Walter took a deep breath and opened both barn doors. There sat Tank's truck, gleaming like new in the morning sun.

Not a smudge.

Not a fingerprint.

Not one little speck of dust.

He ran his hand lightly over the fender.

Over the orange flames on the side.

Across the lightning bolt on the tailgate.

"You gonna drive this thing or pet it like a dang dog?" Banjo said, but then added, "Nice truck, by the way."

Walter opened the door and climbed into the driver's seat.

"You sure you don't want me to drive?" Banjo asked.

Walter nodded. "I'm sure."

He was certain that this was what Tank would've wanted.

For him to be brave.

For him to not let anyone else drive his truck.

149

Posey got in the passenger side and motioned for Porkchop to sit on her lap. Then Banjo climbed in, wheezing and grunting as he lifted his dirty blue cast into the truck.

Walter took the keys out of the glove compartment, put them in the ignition, and started the engine. The country music Tank had loved so much blasted out of the radio.

Banjo reached over and turned it off. "You want everybody in Harmony to hear us coming?" he said.

Walter pushed himself closer to the steering wheel. If he sat way up on the edge of the seat, he could reach the gas pedal with his toes. Then he checked to make sure he could also reach the brake.

He carefully put the gear in reverse.

He lightly pressed on the gas.

The truck began to move.

Back, back, back.

Until it was completely out of the barn.

He closed his eyes and took a deep breath.

Then he opened his eyes, turned to Posey and Banjo, and said, "Let's do this!"

TWENTY-EIGHT

"Will you close the barn doors, Banjo?" Walter said.

"Naw, just go." Banjo waved a hand at him.

"Look," Walter said. "If we're not back before Mama and Evalina get home, at least the barn doors will be closed and they won't catch on right away." He glanced anxiously at the barn. "*But*," he added. "We've *got* to be back before them."

Posey nudged Banjo with her elbow. "He's right. Go close the doors."

Banjo struggled out of the truck, mumbling under his breath, and closed the barn doors.

When he got back into the truck, Posey started singing, with Porkchop wiggling excitedly on her lap. "*Off we go, into the wild blue yonder!*"

"Be quiet!" Walter snapped. "I need to concentrate."

Posey clamped her mouth shut and shot him a glare.

"Sorry," Walter said. He craned his neck to see out the rearview mirror as he backed up more. He put the gear in drive and drove around to the back of the barn. Sure enough, there was a clearing in the woods wide enough for the truck to get through.

Walter drove slowly through the woods, every now and then bumping over a fallen branch or driving over clusters of scrawny bushes. As the truck bounced along, that horseshoe necklace on the rearview mirror swung back and forth.

They hadn't gone far when they reached a logging road.

"I'm pretty sure we go left here," Walter said. "There should be another road that heads toward the river."

The three of them sat silently in the truck as they made their way along the narrow, overgrown dirt roads.

Walter strained to see over the steering wheel and reach the gas pedal and brakes, his heart pounding with fear and his stomach churning with excitement.

He could hardly believe he was really doing this.

Driving Tank's truck through the woods.

He was certain Tank would've been proud.

Would've slapped him on the back and said, "Way to go, little man!"

Every now and then, the side of the truck would scrape against scrub pines or overgrown shrubs tangled with vines and Walter nearly went crazy with worry about scratching his brother's beloved truck.

Finally, they rounded a curve and there in the distance was the river.

Posey bounced up and down on the seat, Porkchop barked gleefully, and Banjo did a little drumroll on the dashboard with his fingers.

Walter drove slowly, trying to dodge overhanging limbs, until they reached a fork in the road.

"The bridge is that way," he said. "I'm thinking *Starcatcher* is not much farther up the side of the river."

A short distance later, he stopped the truck.

"I think *Starcatcher* is somewhere in that direction." He pointed at a clearing in the woods where they could see the river flowing lazily along.

Posey pulled her map out of the pocket of her shorts and opened it up. "I think you're right!" she said. "Let's go!"

They scrambled out of the truck and hurried toward

the river, with Porkchop racing ahead of them in that three-legged hopping way of his.

At least, Walter and Posey hurried.

Banjo, of course, hobbled after them, calling, "Goldern it! Wait up!"

Walter's heart raced as he stood by the river's edge.

"There it is!" he hollered, hurrying up the riverbank until he reached the spot where he and Posey had secured the balloon to the trees and shrubs. Porkchop was already there, barking excitedly.

Posey raced after them, letting out a few loud cheers that echoed across the water.

Finally, Banjo reached them, huffing and puffing and brushing dirt off his toes sticking out of the cast.

The three of them looked at one another, grinning.

They had done it!

Plowed around the stumps.

At least most of the stumps.

They still had two big stumps left to plow around.

Two very big stumps.

They had to get the balloon to Banjo's house.

Then they had to get Tank's truck safely back in the barn before Mama and Evalina got home.

TWENTY-NINE

Getting the balloon into the back of Tank's truck was harder than they thought it would be.

Banjo was practically useless. He stood on the riverbank reminding Walter and Posey that he couldn't get his cast wet.

It was up to them to untie the balloon from the shrubs and the basket from the tree and then figure out what to do next.

"Let's fold this end over there," Walter said.

Posey shook her head. "No, it'd be better if we unhooked the basket and then—"

"But if we unhook the basket, we'll have to tie it to the tree again 'cause the river will—"

Back and forth they went, each one having a different idea while Banjo barked orders at them.

"Naw, you two, not like that!"

"For criminey's sake, untie the other end!"

"Walter! Walter! Walter! Stop a minute!"

And so it went.

A bit of chaos.

Porkchop raced back and forth in the shallow water
at the edge of the river, splashing Banjo with muddy
water and making him holler, "Stop that, you flea-bitten
mutt!"

Walter was getting more and more frustrated and
then Posey went and made things worse by reminding
him about those friend-making rules of Caesar
Romanoff's.

"Have you forgotten rule number five?" she said.
"Quit your griping."

Walter shot her a dirty look.

"And I went in that nasty, snake-infested water to
pull that basket out," Posey told him. "You could try
remembering rule number eight and thank me, you
know."

"We never got to rule number eight," Walter snapped.

They both grunted and panted and pushed and pulled until, finally, they had done it.

The wet, muddy fabric of the balloon was folded into a large, messy rectangle and the wicker basket was well out of the water and resting on its side on the riverbank.

Posey plopped down on the ground, then flopped back against the rocky slope and draped her arm over her eyes. "Okay, *Jubilation*," she said loudly. "Now you've got to help us get this thing in the truck. Need I remind you that this is *your* balloon?"

"Need I remind *you*," Banjo said, "that I am an injured man. Disabled by the weight of this cast and infused with the pain that surges from these bruised and battered toes of mine clear up through my gullet to my head, leaving me with a throbbing headache the likes of which I would not wish upon even the mortalest of my enemies. Not even that good-for-nothing Kudzu."

"Okay, look, y'all," Walter said. "We've got to hurry. Mama and Evalina will be coming back from town and we still have to get the balloon to Banjo's and get Tank's truck home."

Banjo helped Walter and Posey take a part of the

folded-up balloon fabric, drag it to the truck, and heave it into the back. Then they returned for the basket, which proved harder to drag and harder still to get into the truck.

But they did it.

Then they climbed in and Walter drove slowly along the logging road to the Chattahoochee bridge.

When he got to the main road, he stopped.

His stomach did a flip when he realized a car was coming up the road toward them.

And there he sat, an almost-eleven-year-old boy driving a pickup truck.

His heart began to pound.

His hands began to shake.

He put the gear in park and took a few deep breaths.

Suddenly Banjo was pushing the back of his head.

"Get down!" he hollered. "Pretend like you're looking for something on the floor."

Walter ducked down and stared at his wet sneaker on the brake.

The mud and rocks on the floorboard.

Posey's dirty rubber boots.

What had he done?

Here he was driving Tank's truck, probably about to get taken to jail any minute.

And the sight of the mud and rocks on the floor of the truck made him feel sick. He could only imagine what the rest of the truck looked like.

He let out a groan.

"Keep quiet and stay down," Banjo said.

"There's another car coming," Posey said.

Walter groaned again and closed his eyes.

Finally, after what felt like forever, Banjo tapped him on the shoulder.

"Coast is clear," he said.

Walter sat up, blinking. "Now what?"

"Now give her some gas and head straight for that field over yonder," Banjo said.

That meant driving across the highway.

Walter put the gear in drive.

He closed his eyes and listened to his thumping heart.

He couldn't do it.

But he *had* to do it.

They had come this far.

He couldn't give up now.

He opened his eyes and looked both ways.

Then looked both ways again.

No cars in either direction.

He held his breath and stomped on the gas.

The truck shot across the road and into the field on the other side.

He stopped and clamped a hand on his heart. "I did it!"

"Don't stop now, you nimrod!" Banjo yelled. "Go, go, go!" He waved his hands wildly toward the field in front of them.

Walter drove the truck through the field that looked like it had once been farmland but was now only wildflowers, milkweed, and scrub pines.

He drove and drove, the truck bouncing and bumping through the field, that horseshoe necklace swinging wildly, until suddenly, Banjo pointed and yelled, "Stop! Go that way!"

Walter drove in that direction and before long the field became red dirt and there in front of them was a ramshackle house. Beside the ramshackle house was a sun-faded, leaning barn.

"There it is!" Banjo said. "Casa de Jubilation. Château de Fairweather. My humble and welcoming abode."

"What do we do now?" Walter asked.

"We put my beloved balloon in the barn and then we will have successfully driven around one monster of a stump," Banjo said.

So that's what they did.

The three of them pulled and pushed and panted and grunted until the folded fabric and the wicker basket were safely inside Banjo's barn.

They slapped high fives and Posey said, "Mission accomplished!"

"Mission accomplished!" Banjo said.

But Walter's smile faded.

"Not quite," he said. "We still have to get Tank's truck back home."

THIRTY

Walter gripped the steering wheel and stared straight ahead.

He had done this before.

He would do it again.

He would drive the truck over the bumpy field.

Across the highway.

Through the maze of dirt logging roads.

Along the narrow pathway to the barn.

Around the barn and then, hallelujah, safely *into* the barn.

He would close the barn doors and breathe a sigh of relief.

But for now, he gripped the steering wheel and stared straight ahead.

He was barely aware of Posey and Banjo cheering him on.

"Way to go, Walter!"

"Attaboy, Walter!"

Even Porkchop wagged his tail as he sat on Posey's lap.

Walter was so completely exhausted it was all he could do to keep from getting out of the truck and dropping to the ground to sleep forever.

He felt Posey poking him in the leg.

He shook his head and looked at her.

"Let's go!" she said. "We've gotta beat Evalina and your mama, remember?"

Walter blinked at her. "Right."

He took a deep breath and stepped on the gas.

The truck bounced along back through the field until it came to the highway by the bridge.

All three of them looked both ways.

No cars.

"Let's get 'er done!" Banjo hollered.

Off they went, across the highway toward the river.

Then Walter turned onto the logging road and began to make his way back home. But a short time later, Posey sat up ramrod straight and said, "Wait! Stop! This isn't right." She took out her map and squinted down at it. "I think we need to go that way," she said.

Walter wasn't so sure, but he remembered that geography was one of Posey's specialties.

He turned the truck around, which was not so easy to do on the narrow road and required Banjo to get out of the truck and direct him. Grumbling, of course.

But eventually they came to the wide path that led to the back of Walter's barn.

As he turned onto the path, Walter's stomach finally began to settle down and he realized that he was actually smiling.

When the back of the barn came into view, he stopped the truck.

"*Now*," he said, "mission accomplished!"

They grinned and fist-bumped, and Banjo said, "This is one fine and glorious day."

Then Walter drove slowly along the side of the barn.

But when he turned the corner, there in front of them was a terrible sight.

Walter's father's car was parked in the driveway beside the barn.

THIRTY-ONE

Walter slammed on the brakes so hard that Posey and Banjo were thrown forward with a jolt.

Posey whipped her head sideways to look at Walter, her eyes narrowed, her face red, and her mouth ready to give him what-for. But when she saw his face, she froze. She looked over at the car in the driveway, then back at Walter.

"Whose car is that?" she asked.

But Walter couldn't speak.

He couldn't move.

He couldn't even think.

He just sat there feeling queasy, his hands gripping the steering wheel and his heart pounding.

"What in tarnation is going on?" Banjo asked.

Then the back door of Walter's house opened and out stepped a man.

A man with an angry face.

A very angry face.

"Hello, Walter," he said.

Somehow Walter managed to get himself to move. He put the truck in park and took his foot off the brake. He turned the ignition off and dropped his hands to his lap. He rolled down the window.

His shoulders slumped.

His eyes looked down.

"Hey, Daddy," he mumbled.

Mr. Tipple walked over to the truck and leaned in through the open driver's-side window.

"Wanna introduce me to your friends?" he said.

"Um, Posey and Banjo," Walter answered, still looking down.

"Look at me," Mr. Tipple said.

Walter did.

It was hard, but he did.

His face was burning.

His hands were trembling.

"Why don't y'all get out of that truck and tell me what's going on?" Mr. Tipple said.

Walter and Posey and Banjo and Porkchop got out of the truck and everyone started telling Mr. Tipple what was going on. But Mr. Tipple held up a hand and said, "Whoa, now. One at a time."

Banjo went first, telling Mr. Tipple about his bodacious adventure in that grand and dramatic way of his. He ended by proclaiming Walter one of the finest young men that ever walked the beloved red-dirt ground of the great state of Georgia and beyond.

Posey went next, starting at the part where she and Walter had thought they had found a dead man in the woods and how good Walter was at *Caesar Romanoff's Rules for Making Friends*.

Porkchop sat by the truck, his tail going swish, swish, swish in the dirt.

Banjo and Posey and Mr. Tipple looked at Walter.

Walter cleared his throat.

He looked his father square in the eyes and told him everything.

How Posey had moved in next door with Evalina a week and a half ago.

How Banjo had fallen out of the sky and broken his ankle and wanted to win a new truck in the hot-air balloon key-grab competition over in Macon County.

How he and Posey had found the balloon in the river.

How Banjo's truck had broken down and they had to get the balloon before something happened to it.

And then, the hardest part of all—how he had gotten the idea to drive Tank's truck to the river to get the balloon.

And then Walter surprised himself.

He started telling his father things he had never said out loud before.

"I been missing Tank a lot, Daddy," he said. "Sometimes I can practically hear him talking to me." He swallowed hard, trying to clear the lump in his throat. "When I decided to take his truck to the river, I was really scared, but I wanted to be like Tank, even if just for one day. I swear I heard Tank say, 'You got this, little man. You can do it.'"

He looked up at his father. "And I did it! I drove Tank's truck to the river to get Banjo's balloon."

Walter felt blanketed in silence except for the sound of his beating heart.

Then he felt his father's warm hand on his shoulder and a heavy weight lifted up off him because that warm hand told him that maybe everything was going to be okay.

THIRTY-TWO

Walter sat on the couch and stared down at his shoes while his mother and father told him how disappointed in him they were.

They had been so surprised he would do such a foolish thing.

What was he thinking?

Did he have any idea how serious this was? A ten-year-old boy driving a *truck*? And with two passengers?

He could have hurt someone.

Or worse.

And what about the truck?

Had he even *thought* about the fact that he could have damaged the truck?

Walter said *yessir* and *no, ma'am* in all the right places.

Every now and then, his mother mumbled words like *outrageous* and *ridiculous*. A few times she snapped something about that nut Banjo and how she never should've left Walter home with him.

As Walter listened, a little bubble of anger began to form inside him.

It grew and grew until it burst and the next thing Walter knew he was yelling.

At his parents!

He never yelled at his parents.

But now loud, angry words came spilling out.

He couldn't stop them.

He told his parents all the things that had been eating him up inside ever since Tank died.

How his father just went on back to work like nothing had happened, leaving him and Mama home in this silent house.

How Mama was so sad and grumpy most of the time and made macaroni and cheese from a box.

Didn't she even care that he, Walter Tipple, loved her homemade macaroni and cheese as much as Tank had?

And she never laughed anymore. Sure, he wasn't as funny as Tank had been, but still, maybe she could smile once in a while.

Then he got to the icing on the cake.

He stood in front of his mother and said, "And then you cleaned all of Tank's stuff out of his bedroom and put it out in the barn like those things are just nothing." He said it a little louder than he probably should have. "The football trophies and the fake leather jacket and everything," he continued. "And now it's like Tank never lived here and y'all don't even care."

His eyes burned with tears and he added, "So I guess y'all don't even care about me, either."

When he finally stopped talking, he took a good look at his mother's face and felt a wave of guilt.

She looked shocked and sad and hurt all rolled into one.

Silence fell over the room.

His father cleared his throat.

His mother twisted a tissue around a finger and looked in the direction of Tank's room.

She stood up and put her arm around Walter.

"I'm sorry," she said. "I care about you more than

you could ever know. I guess I've been missing Tank so much I wasn't thinking about anything else."

Walter closed his eyes. "I miss him, too, you know," he said.

"I'll try to do better," his mother said. "I'll make real macaroni and cheese tonight."

Walter couldn't help but smile a little at that.

"I'll see if I can be home more," his father said.

Just as Walter was starting to feel a teeny bit better, his father added, "But you know there have to be consequences for taking that truck like you did."

Then he handed down Walter's sentence.

Grounded for a week.

Inside the house or in the yard only.

Doing chores.

No Posey.

No Porkchop.

No Banjo.

No fun.

Walter's mind raced. A week? When was that hot-air balloon key-grab competition? He couldn't miss it. He heaved a big silent sigh of relief when he realized that the competition was a little more than a week away. The day after his birthday, as a matter of fact.

His thoughts were interrupted when his father told him to get outside and clean every inch of Tank's truck, inside and out, until it looked brand-spanking-new.

Walter put one heavy foot in front of the other as he made his way toward the door.

But before he stepped out onto the porch, his father came over and put his hand on Walter's shoulder.

"Tank would've been proud of you," he said.

A lot of heavy weight lifted when Walter heard that.

Not all of it.

But a lot of it.

Outside, Walter's heart squeezed up at the sight of Tank's truck. He had been so scared and nervous when he'd gotten out of the truck earlier that he hadn't even noticed.

Instead of being spotless and shiny, the truck was covered with dirt and dust.

The doors and fenders were scratched.

Not bad.

But still . . .

Walter licked a finger and rubbed at one of the scratches. He was pretty sure he could use Tank's electric buffer and some car wax and those scratches would be gone.

174

He opened the door and peered inside. Dirt and pebbles and leaves. Nothing that Tank's Shop-Vac couldn't take care of.

Walter got right to work.

He washed and buffed and rubbed and vacuumed and swept until the truck looked perfect, inside and out.

Then he climbed into the driver's seat and said, "Hey, Tank. I did it!"

And he could have sworn he heard Tank say, "Way to go, little man!"

THIRTY-THREE

That week was the longest one of Walter's life.

He weeded the garden.

He cleaned the chicken house.

He helped his father straighten the mailbox that had been leaning for so long.

He washed window screens.

He hung curtains on the clothesline after his mother washed them.

He ironed fabric for the quilt his mother was making with Evalina.

He had no fun at all.

Banjo finally got the part he needed to fix his truck and Walter was at least allowed to watch from the porch as Banjo turned the key and that rattletrap of a truck started with a rumble while puffs of black smoke drifted from the tailpipe into the summer sky.

Banjo had leaned out the window and hollered, "Adios, amigos! Until we meet again!"

Posey and Evalina waved from their porch and Mama gave a half-hearted wave from her chair by the garden. Banjo's rusty old truck chugged down the gravel road with Porkchop hop-trotting along behind it until it disappeared up the highway, leaving Walter alone with his chores.

Every now and then, Posey would sneak over and whisper to him outside his bedroom window. Evalina had read Posey the riot act for her part in Banjo's Bodacious Adventure, but at least Posey wasn't grounded like Walter.

Sometimes she read some nuggets of knowledge to him.

"What size was the biggest whale ever caught?" she asked.

Of course Walter couldn't answer so she didn't even wait. "Seventy-five feet long," she said. "What state is known as the Mother of Presidents because so many presidents were born there?"

"Um . . ."

"Take a guess."

"Pennsylvania."

"Nope. Virginia."

"What's going on with Banjo and *Starcatcher*?" Walter asked.

Posey filled him in.

Banjo called often to tell Evalina his progress. He was busy repairing the fabric, sewing up the tears with his heavy-duty sewing machine.

One of the metal tanks that held the propane gas that made the balloon rise had gotten dented pretty bad, so Banjo was trying to find another one in time for the key grab.

Posey stuck her face up close to the window screen and said, "We have *got* to go to that key grab."

Walter nodded solemnly. "I know."

"How much longer are you stuck in prison?"

"Three more days."

Posey snapped her fingers. "That's perfect!" she said. "The key grab is next Wednesday."

"But maybe I won't be allowed to go," Walter said.

Posey stamped her foot. "Oh, good grief, Walter. Remember Caesar Romanoff's rule number one?"

"Think positive," Walter mumbled.

The next day, Walter's mother said, "Would you like to invite Posey and Evalina over for cake on your birthday?"

"Um, yeah, sure," Walter said. "And Banjo?"

His mother scowled, then sighed. "Sure, if you want to," she said. "Have you thought about what you might like? For a present, I mean."

Walter didn't have to think long.

"I'd like to go watch Banjo in the Macon County Key Grab next week," he said.

His mother's face grew serious. "I don't know, Walter," she said. "Seems like you got yourself into a heap of trouble with Banjo and that balloon."

"I know, but . . ."

His mother held up a finger. "Let me talk to your daddy. But I can't promise anything." Then she gave Walter the hug that he'd been needing.

THIRTY-FOUR

The night before his birthday, Walter had that dream again.

Only this time, a few things were different.

For one, Posey, Evalina, and Banjo were in it. And Porkchop.

Everyone sang "Happy Birthday" and then, just like before, Tank came bursting through the front door in his army uniform.

And like before, he threw his arms out and said, "Look who's back!"

He took off his army hat, plunked it down on Walter's head, and said, "Blow out them candles, little man, and I'll show you my world." He slapped Walter on the back and added, "But you gotta blow 'em *all* out. First try. No cheating."

He grinned that chipped-tooth grin of his.

Then he crossed his arms and tapped his foot and said, "I ain't got all day."

But this time in the dream, Walter looked down at those eleven candles, took a deep breath . . .

. . . and blew them all out.

First try.

Tank slung his arm over Walter's shoulder and said, "Good job. Let's you and me go see my world, little man."

Then Walter woke up.

He lay there in the dark, blinking up at the ceiling, thinking about the dream.

Maybe Posey was right. Maybe that dream was just a little blip of feel-good he'd been needing in his otherwise sorry existence.

A wave of contentment settled over him, soft and warm.

A feeling he hadn't had in a long time.

It swirled around him and then inside him, pushing away some of the sadness that had seemed to take root when Tank died.

Not *all* of it.

But some of it.

His birthday was finally here.

The birthday he'd been dreaming about so many nights since Tank left.

Walter wandered around the house, every once in a while glancing at the clock. He could almost swear those clock hands weren't moving one bit.

Finally, Posey and Evalina arrived with Porkchop trotting along behind them. Mr. and Mrs. Tipple greeted them and they gathered around the kitchen table, admiring Walter's birthday cake. Chocolate cake with his mama's buttercream frosting.

"Ta-da!" Posey said, handing Walter a small spiral-bound notebook.

Written neatly on the cover in blue marker was *Caesar Romanoff's Rules for Making Friends*.

"Wow!" Walter said. "Thanks." He thumbed through the pages. Posey had written a rule on each page.

"It's not all of them," she said. "But I'm pretty sure it's most of them." She beamed proudly. "I have practically a photographic memory," she reminded Walter.

Suddenly the sound of chugging and rumbling and sputtering got louder and louder outside.

"Banjo!" Walter hollered, racing to the front door, while Porkchop ran around in circles barking.

Banjo came hobbling up the front steps in his dirty blue cast and threw his arms out wide.

"Happy birthday, Walter Tipple!" he said. "Congratulations for making yet another trip around the sun. In celebration, I present to you this treasure, given to me by some ne'er-do-well who had the audacity to think he could beat me at Texas hold'em, a game at which I mightily excel."

He reached into the pocket of his overalls and pulled out three shiny silver dollars and handed them to Walter.

"Wow! Thanks, Banjo," Walter said.

Then Walter's mother lit the eleven candles on the cake and led them all in singing "Happy Birthday."

Walter couldn't shake the feeling that he was dreaming. That he was going to wake up any minute.

He stared down at the burning candles and could have sworn he heard Tank say, "But you gotta blow 'em *all* out. First try. No cheating."

He gave his head a little shake, trying to clear his mind.

What if he *didn't* blow out all the candles on the first try?

But that was just a dream, right?

It didn't mean anything, did it?

Suddenly he remembered he was supposed to make a wish.

He looked up at the ceiling.

He only had one wish.

He wished he would blow out all those candles on the first try.

He closed his eyes, took a deep breath, and blew out all the candles.

Later that evening, Banjo limped back to his truck. But before getting in, he made an announcement.

"Tomorrow, good people, I will win the Macon County Key Grab. And I will do it while piloting my beloved hot-air balloon, newly christened . . ."

He bowed a big, dramatic bow, sweeping off an invisible hat and holding it over his heart.

"Newly christened . . . *Evalina*!"

"Oh, brother," Posey said.

Evalina blushed and even giggled a little.

"And I would be proud and honored if the name-sake of my beloved balloon would accompany me to that key grab."

Posey pumped her fist. "Yes!" she said.

Evalina stammered and stuttered a little and finally said yes, she would love to go to the Macon County Key Grab.

"I'll bring Posey and Walter with me," she said.

Walter looked anxiously at his parents. "Can I go?" he asked.

Please, please, please, he said in his head.

Then much to his relief, his father nodded.

"Sure," he said. Then he ruffled Walter's hair and said, "Happy birthday, Walter."

After everyone had left, Walter went out to sit in Tank's truck to let his feelings settle down a bit.

Sad and mad.

Swirling around together and weighing him down.

Sad that Tank was gone.

Sad to have his first birthday without his brother.

But still mad that Tank hadn't even come home to say goodbye before he went overseas like he said he would.

And mad that he had seemed so happy to be leaving Harmony.

Which meant leaving Walter behind.

Walter took the envelope out of the glove box and put it on the seat beside him. He stared down at Tank's messy handwriting.

Walter Tipple scrawled in blue ink.

He sighed a big heaving sigh and put the envelope away. Someday he would open it.

But not today.

Not on his birthday.

This letter might be like all the others, telling Walter how great it was to be so far from Harmony.

He pushed aside his bad feelings and let excitement settle in. Tomorrow was the Macon County Key Grab and he would finally see Banjo's beautiful balloon floating above him in the Georgia sky.

THIRTY-FIVE

Walter opened his eyes and looked at the clock.

Midnight.

He closed his eyes.

Sleep, sleep, sleep, he told himself.

But too much excitement was tumbling around inside him.

Tomorrow, Evalina would take Posey and him to the Macon County Key Grab in Oakley, Georgia, almost a half hour's drive up County Road 19 from Harmony. Banjo had explained that the competition would start at sunrise, when the air was most stable, making conditions better for flying the balloons, so they should plan on leaving no later than six o'clock that morning.

Walter opened his eyes again.

It was 12:28.

This was going to be a long night.

But he must have fallen asleep eventually, because the next time he looked at the clock it was five thirty.

He sprang out of bed, got dressed in the dark, and hurried out to the kitchen.

Mama was there in her bathrobe, making blueberry pancakes. "It sure is nice of Evalina to drive y'all clear over to Oakley," she said.

"I know," Walter said. "And I bet Banjo wins that key grab, don't you?"

His mother chuckled. "Well, if being stubborn and determined is what it takes to win, I'd say Banjo is a sure thing."

While Walter gobbled down the pancakes, Mama put bologna sandwiches and four slices of birthday cake into a grocery bag.

"Have fun," she said, giving Walter a hug.

"Thanks." Walter grabbed the bag and raced out the door.

Outside, darkness and silence were still settled peacefully over the yard. The sweet scent of honeysuckle floated in the summer air and the grass was damp with dew.

Posey was already waiting in the front seat of Evalina's car, with Porkchop on her lap. She motioned to Walter through the open window.

"I brought pickles," she said, holding up a jar.

Walter climbed into the back seat and he and Posey sat in the darkness, waiting for Evalina. Posey chattered on and on about stuff she had read in *Land, Sea, and Air: A Child's Book About Transportation*, but Walter wasn't really listening. He was trying to picture Banjo's balloon, drifting above them.

Every color of the rainbow with silver stars and golden moons.

Finally, Evalina came out, yawning and sipping coffee from a mug. "Okay, y'all," she said. "Let's go!"

The drive to Oakley seemed to take forever, but finally they pulled into the empty fairgrounds where the key grab would start. As they were getting out of the car, Banjo came limping toward them.

"Greetings and salutations, dear ones," he called. "Meet my friend, Lady Luck." He motioned to an invisible person beside him. "She came knocking on my door when the roosters crowed this morning and I welcomed her with open arms."

"What does that mean?" Posey asked.

189

"Means I've got luck on my side this fine morning," Banjo said. "I plan on driving y'all to lunch in my brand-new Ford F-150 pickup truck."

"Mama made bologna sandwiches," Walter said, holding up the grocery bag.

"Bologna sandwiches?" Banjo said. "No offense, but bologna sandwiches are for peasants. Y'all will be treated to a feast of the finest foods the metropolis of Oakley has to offer." He turned to Evalina and added, "The first of many fine feasts I hope to share with the lovely Evalina."

He motioned toward the fairgrounds. "Shall we?" he said, leading the way.

Everywhere Walter looked there were deflated hot-air balloons spread out flat on the ground. Every color and pattern imaginable.

Each balloon had a wicker basket attached and lying on its side, while people hustled and bustled around, preparing for the start of the competition.

Finally, they got to Banjo's balloon.

Walter's heart leaped at the sight of it. The silky fabric was still a little dirty in spots, but Banjo had done a good job repairing the tears and snags caused by the trees and shrubs along the river. And there was something new about the balloon. Bright yellow fabric letters spelled out *Evalina* on the side.

Suddenly someone hollered, "Hey, Jubilation!"

Walking toward them was a man with a scruffy red beard.

"You're late," Banjo snapped irritably.

"Well, good morning to you, too, Jubilation," the man said.

Banjo nodded toward him. "This is my friend Kudzu showing up an hour late to be my one-man ground crew."

He put his arm around Evalina's shoulder. "*This* is the fine, fair maiden who was sent from heaven to sweeten my world with her very existence," he told Kudzu.

Posey did one of her eye rolls and Evalina blushed and shook hands with the bushy-bearded Kudzu.

Banjo pointed to Walter and Posey. "These two miniature humans are Posey and Walter," he said. "The ones who took it upon themselves to find my beloved balloon, newly christened *Evalina*."

He nodded toward Porkchop, who was sniffing Kudzu's muddy sneakers and growling. "That there is Porkchop, the feistiest three-legged varmint you'll ever meet."

When Porkchop heard his name, his head shot up and he let out a yip.

Banjo explained how the competition would begin here at the fairgrounds. The balloons would go several miles to the Oakley High School football field, where the keys to the truck would be attached to the top of a goalpost. He, of course, would then maneuver his balloon perfectly and be the first one there to grab the keys.

"Easy peasy," Banjo said. "Kudzu will drive y'all to the high school to witness my victory." He turned to face Evalina and looked imploringly into her eyes. "*However*, I would like to extend an invitation to you, Miss Evalina, to accompany me on my glorious ride to victory, otherwise known as my bodacious adventure."

What?

Walter couldn't believe it.

Banjo was inviting Evalina to ride in the balloon!

What about him and Posey?

Posey started snapping, "No fair" and "Why her?" and "What about me and Walter?"

But before Walter could join in, Evalina began to shake her head.

"No way," she said. "I'm scared of two things on this earth. Snakes being one and heights being the other."

"Miss Evalina can wait down here with me," Kudzu said, smiling at Evalina. "I will take care of her every need like the fine Southern gentleman that I am."

Banjo's face turned red. "My dear, dear Evalina. You cannot soar with the eagles if you hang out with the turkeys," he said, glaring at Kudzu. "Are you sure I can't change your mind?"

"Sorry, Jubilation," Evalina said. "My feet are staying on the ground."

"Me and Posey will go," Walter said. "Right, Posey?"

"Right," Posey said. "Besides, you *owe* me and Walter a ride. That balloon wouldn't even be here if it wasn't for us."

Banjo scratched his chin and glanced over at the balloon, then back at Walter and Posey.

"I guess y'all got a point," he said. "Then prepare yourselves for one bodacious adventure."

Posey whooped and cheered.

Walter whooped and cheered.

Today was going to be a day he had needed for a long, long time.

A bodacious adventure.

THIRTY-SIX

"Let's get cracking," Banjo said. "We gotta get this balloon ready for liftoff. Walter and Posey, y'all just wait here until I tell you it's time to get in the basket."

Walter, Posey, and Evalina watched as Banjo and Kudzu got to work.

Kudzu grabbed a long rope that was attached to the balloon and tied it to the bumper of Banjo's truck.

"Safety line," he explained. "To keep the balloon from floating off before we're ready."

Banjo turned on a large fan that blew air into the balloon.

Slowly the balloon began to fill and before long, it really did look like a balloon instead of just silky fabric on the ground.

It was beautiful.

Every color of the rainbow with silver stars and golden moons.

And of course, *Evalina* in giant yellow letters on the side.

Posey kept rattling off stuff she had learned from *Land, Sea, and Air: A Child's Book About Transportation*.

But Walter wasn't listening.

He was mesmerized by the sight of that balloon filling with air.

While Kudzu scrambled to hold another one of the dangling safety lines, Banjo crawled into the wicker basket, which was still lying on its side.

When the balloon was completely filled, Banjo pushed a small lever on the burner at the top of the basket frame. Suddenly a loud blast of a flame shot out into the balloon.

"That heats the air inside the balloon," Posey explained, lifting her chin proudly. "And everybody knows that hot air rises, right?"

Again and again, Banjo pushed the lever on the burner.

Again and again, a loud *whoosh* of a flame shot into the balloon.

And slowly . . .

Slowly . . .

Slowly . . .

The balloon began to rise up off the ground and hover over the basket, which gradually tilted upward until it was sitting upright, with Banjo standing inside it.

Kudzu pulled hard on the safety cord, keeping the balloon steady.

"Okay, y'all," Banjo called. "Climb in!"

Posey scooped up Porkchop, and she and Walter raced over to the basket.

"Whoa, now, Miss Posey," Banjo said. "You can't bring that mongrel. He'll be yipping and yapping and irritating me. I do *not* need to be irritated on my bodacious adventure."

"I'll tell him to be quiet," Posey said. "You won't even know he's there."

Banjo scowled at Porkchop. "Then y'all get on in here, if you're coming."

Posey grinned at Banjo and carefully placed Porkchop in the basket and climbed in after him.

Walter climbed in, his heart pounding.

He glanced around him and could hardly believe his

eyes. All the other balloons at the fairground were filled with air like Banjo's.

Striped ones.

Checkered ones.

Balloons with butterflies.

Balloons with hearts.

And so many bright, beautiful colors.

Posey kept saying, "Whoa!"

Porkchop barked a couple of times, but Posey quickly told him to hush.

Walter couldn't even speak. He thought he might burst from the thrill of it all.

"Y'all keep an eye on that man in the red cap on top of that truck up yonder," Banjo said, pointing. "He's going to blow an air horn and that means it's liftoff time."

Walter watched the man in the red cap, his heart racing.

Suddenly the shrill sound of the air horn signaled the start of the Macon County Key Grab and everyone cheered.

Kudzu dropped the line he had been holding and raced to untie the other line from the bumper of the truck.

Banjo pushed the lever.

Flames whooshed upward.

And that balloon began to rise slowly off the ground.

Up.

Up.

Up.

Walter looked down and saw Evalina and Kudzu waving excitedly below them.

They grew smaller and smaller as the balloon rose higher.

All around them, the other balloons rose, too, until it seemed like the whole sky was filled with colorful balloons, their whooshing flames flashing in the still-dark morning sky like giant fireflies.

Slowly they began to drift higher and farther until before long, Evalina and Kudzu were nothing but tiny dots and the fairgrounds disappeared behind them.

Eventually Banjo pushed the lever less and less and the other balloons drifted farther away from one another and the most amazing thing happened.

They were swallowed up in silence.

Complete and total silence.

And they floated slowly along in the gentle August breeze.

Every now and then, the balloon would begin to

drop ever so slightly until Banjo pushed the lever and the whooshing flame lifted them up again.

The dark sky began to lighten to pale blue with streaks of rose.

Everything around Walter disappeared except that soft, rosy sky.

No Posey.

No Porkchop.

No Banjo.

No whooshing flame.

There seemed to be nothing but Walter, alone in the sky as the balloon drifted silently on.

Ever so slowly, the sky grew lighter and there on the horizon was the sun, just beginning to rise, as if it were peeking at them from the edge of the earth.

The sun rose higher and higher, turning the sky around it a brilliant orange.

And then the sun was completely visible and the sky was the loveliest, softest blue.

The balloon continued to drift in the breeze.

Every once in a while came the *whoosh* of the flame, lifting them a little higher.

As if by magic, fluffy white clouds appeared around them.

Walter felt as if he could reach right out and touch them.

Once in a while, the balloon floated right through a low-hanging cloud and they were briefly swallowed up in a cool fog.

Finally, for the first time, Walter looked down over the edge of the basket to the ground far below.

He drew in his breath at the sight.

The tops of pine trees.

Ribbons of roads meandering through the countryside.

Fields of corn.

Tiny houses perched here and there.

Underneath them, flocks of birds flew with outstretched wings.

In the distance, miniature traces of small Georgia towns dotted this amazing world below him.

Then Walter suddenly realized the whooshing flames were not as frequent and the balloon was sinking ever so slowly downward.

THIRTY-SEVEN

"There it is!" Banjo hollered.

Sure enough, the Oakley High School football field had finally come into view not far in front of them.

Walter and Posey cheered.

"Okay, Jubilation," Posey said, "go get your new truck!"

"That is precisely what I plan to do." Banjo's face had *confidence* written all over it.

Walter turned away from them both, because he was worried that his face had *skeptical* written all over it.

This competition suddenly seemed a lot harder than he'd thought it would be.

For one thing, there were balloons floating around them.

Beside them.

Under them.

Over them.

Each one heading for those truck keys on the goalpost in the football field.

For another thing, could Banjo really maneuver his balloon so it came down ahead of the others and lined up so perfectly that he could reach out and grab those keys?

Posey had explained to him that Banjo couldn't steer the balloon like a car. The only thing Banjo's balloon could do was drift along in the direction of the wind. And the only way to maneuver the balloon toward the goalpost was to raise and lower it using the whooshing flames.

"Wind direction is different at different altitudes," Posey had explained, but Walter didn't really get it. All he knew was that grabbing those truck keys seemed next to impossible.

Banjo squinted down at the football field, his tongue stuck out of the corner of his mouth. Every few minutes, he pushed the lever to send flames up inside the balloon and it would rise a bit. Before long, it would begin to drop again.

Posey waved her arms frantically, yelling:

202

"Go left! No! Too far! Go right!"

"Quiet!" Banjo snapped. "I need to concentrate."

Down, down, down they drifted, getting closer and closer to the football field.

Several balloons had passed them but hadn't gotten close enough to the goalpost. They dropped slowly down and landed with a bump and a bounce or two onto the football field.

Walter looked around. Some of the balloons had veered off course and were definitely not going anywhere near those keys. But a few of them drifted right alongside Banjo's balloon. Posey waved and smiled at the folks inside them while holding Porkchop.

"Don't be fraternizing with the enemy," Banjo told her.

Walter leaned out of the basket a little and looked up. There was a balloon almost directly over them. A bright yellow balloon with a fire-breathing dragon on the side that began to drop until it grazed the top of Banjo's balloon.

Banjo let out a string of cusswords the likes of which Walter had never heard.

Posey was yelling, "No, not that way! Go more that way!"

Now they were lined up perfectly with the goalpost and continuing to drop.

Down . . .

Down . . .

Down.

The farther they dropped, the more Walter could make out things on the football field below.

People, cars, trucks.

Balloons that had already landed.

"Evalina and Kudzu!" Posey hollered.

Sure enough, Walter could make out Evalina and Kudzu way down below, waving frantically at them.

The dragon balloon above them hit them again, causing Banjo's balloon to drop a little.

Banjo shook his fist, but kept a steady eye on the goalpost not far ahead of them.

Now Walter could actually see the truck keys on a large metal ring hanging from the top of the goalpost.

Suddenly the dragon balloon that had been above them was right beside them.

Banjo glared over at it. Then his eyes grew wide.

"Wiggins Rafferty!" he said.

"Who's that?" Posey asked.

"A highfalutin, good-for-nothing, namby-pamby know-it-all I've had the misfortune to run into from time to time."

Banjo concentrated on guiding the balloon toward the football field while glancing over at the dragon balloon every minute or so.

"He sits around waiting for his daddy to hand him another wad of money," Banjo continued. "He's about as useful as a wooden frying pan." He scowled over at Wiggins Rafferty. "He's got more cars than I got underpants. He will *not*, I repeat, *not* get those truck keys."

But Walter wasn't so sure.

THIRTY-EIGHT

Walter stood, quiet and stiff, gripping the edge of the basket.

Every minute or so, he glanced over at Wiggins Rafferty in the dragon balloon.

"Eat my dust, Banjo Fairweather!" Wiggins yelled over the sound of the whooshing flames.

Banjo's face turned red.

He let a string of not-very-nice names rain down on Wiggins.

Now Walter could hear folks on the football field cheering.

The two balloons drifted closer and closer to the goalpost.

Side by side.

Banjo pushed the lever, releasing a *whoosh* of flame that caused the balloon to rise a little.

Unfortunately, just enough to allow the dragon balloon to inch ahead of them.

"Thanks, Banjo!" Wiggins yelled over at them.

But luck was on Banjo's side. His balloon caught a hint of a breeze to push it almost beside Wiggins's again.

As the two balloons neared the goalpost, it was clear that they would most likely reach it at the same time.

Which was exactly what happened.

Banjo on one side of the goalpost.

Wiggins on the other.

Those keys hanging there between them on a shiny gold ring that glittered in the early-morning sun.

"I'll grab 'em!" Posey said, reaching a hand out of the side of the basket while holding Porkchop with the other.

"Naw," Banjo said. "Let me have my moment of glory."

Posey stepped back and Banjo leaned so far over the edge of the basket that Walter was certain he was going to tumble out and drop like a brick to the ground below.

Fortunately, he didn't.

Unfortunately, Wiggins, too, was leaning far out of the side of his balloon basket with an outstretched arm.

With one quick swipe, Wiggins grabbed the keys and let out a loud "Yeehaw!" that echoed across the football field below them.

He turned and grinned at Banjo, jiggling that shiny gold key ring in the air.

Banjo was so whopping mad that Walter was seriously afraid he was going to keel over from a heart attack.

The veins in his neck bulged.

He stomped his foot.

He banged his fists against the metal frame of the balloon basket.

And he seemed to forget that he was supposed to land in the football field.

Wiggins had already landed the dragon balloon and was surrounded by a cheering crowd, but Banjo was so busy ranting and raving that he let his balloon drift off course, not toward the football field, but toward County Road 19.

The road that led to Harmony.

"Hey!" Posey yelled. "Get a grip, Jubilation. You're going the wrong way!"

"Um, Banjo," Walter said. "We're headed toward the highway."

But Banjo kept ranting about that good-for-nothing, sorry excuse for a human being, Wiggins Rafferty.

Posey set Porkchop down and hauled off and kicked Banjo in the shin.

"Snap out of it!" she hollered.

Banjo howled and grabbed his leg, which left him standing on his ridiculously dirty blue cast, which made him fall right over inside the basket.

Porkchop snarled and snapped at the air in front of Banjo's face.

"Get that three-legged fleabag away from me!" he said.

Posey put her hands on her hips and stood over him. "You're gonna kill us all! Are you gonna fly this balloon or just lay there throwing a tantrum like a two-year-old?"

"Get outta my way," Banjo said, struggling to his feet.

He squinted ahead, surveying the countryside in the distance, then yanked on the lever, sending a whoosh of flame up into the balloon.

Suddenly a gust of wind pushed the balloon faster.

Farther and farther away from Oakley High School.

Posey waved her arms. "You're going the wrong way!"

Walter's heart pounded.

They couldn't go back.

He peered out over the edge of the basket, watching the football field disappear out of sight behind them.

THIRTY-NINE

Below them were roads and power lines and churches and houses.

Not places that seemed good for landing a balloon.

Banjo's eyes darted from side to side, surveying the sights below them. Every now and then, he pushed the lever to send up the flame.

The balloon floated up.

The balloon drifted down.

Farther and farther from Oakley.

"Um, Banjo," Walter said. "Where are we going?"

Banjo stared straight ahead, his twirly mustache blowing in the breeze. "I'm trying to find somewhere to land this thing," he said.

"Where in the heck are we?" Posey asked.

"Well," Banjo said, "near as I can tell, we're halfway to Harmony."

Halfway to Harmony?

Walter clutched the edge of the basket and gazed out at the countryside that stretched ahead of them.

Suddenly his heart nearly leaped right out of his chest.

There in the distance was the water tower with HARMONY painted in red on the side, where Tank and his friends had often hung out in the evenings.

As the wind continued to push them along, he recognized more and more of Harmony.

The steeple of Oak Grove Methodist Church and the parking lot where Tank had let Walter drive his truck.

The Harmony High School football field, where Tank had scored so many touchdowns.

The Chattahoochee River, where Tank had showed Walter the best fishing spots.

And all those narrow country roads where Tank had driven his beloved truck.

Walter was seeing Tank's world there below him, drifting closer and closer.

He closed his eyes.

And heard Tank.

Talking to him.

Clear as anything.

"Ain't this something, little man? You and me seeing my world."

Walter opened his eyes and of course Tank wasn't *really* there.

At least, not so Walter could see or touch him.

But he could *feel* him.

Right there beside him as Harmony drifted along below.

FORTY

Walter's happy thoughts were interrupted by Banjo hollering, "That gol-dern, no-good Kudzu!"

He was frantically pushing the lever but no flames were shooting up into the balloon.

"What's wrong?" Posey asked.

"The tank must be empty and Kudzu didn't put the spare one in the basket." Banjo surveyed the landscape below them.

Walter and Posey gripped the basket and peered out over the edge.

Banjo yelled, "Hold on for dear life! We're going down!"

They all grabbed the metal frame of the basket and held on for dear life.

They were dropping quickly and headed straight for the highway.

As they got closer, cars began to stop, some of them even pulling onto the side of the road.

Banjo's balloon, the newly named *Evalina*, dropped lower and lower until it hit the road with a hard *thump* and bounced a couple of times before coming to a stop and tipping over on its side, sending them tumbling on top of one another.

Porkchop let out a little yelp and Posey scooped him up. "Nice landing, Jubilation," she said, scowling at Banjo, who was huffing and puffing trying to stand up.

Walter scrambled out of the basket, shook his head, and caught his breath.

Banjo pulled a cord that opened a vent at the top of the balloon, releasing the air inside and sending the colorful fabric fluttering down until it lay in a wrinkled heap in the road.

"It's all right, folks!" Banjo said, waving off the crowd that had begun to gather around them. "Nothing to see here. Move along."

Then car horns began to honk and some of the drivers shook their fists and yelled for Banjo to get that contraption out of the road.

Suddenly Kudzu's truck came roaring up the side of the road and stopped with a *screech* beside them.

"What in blue blazes is wrong with you, Banjo?" Kudzu asked. "Why didn't you land at the fairgrounds?"

By now, Banjo was out of the basket and standing in the road, red-faced. He called Kudzu every name in the book and then snapped, "Help me move this thing."

Along with a couple of other folks who had been watching from their cars, they managed to get the balloon onto the side of the road.

It was a very long and very quiet ride back to Oakley with the balloon in the back of Kudzu's truck.

When they got there, Evalina was fighting mad at Banjo and let him have it up one side and down the other.

She was also mad at herself for letting Posey and Walter ride in the balloon.

"What was I *thinking*?" she kept saying on the way back to her car.

"Y'all could've *died*," she reminded them over and over.

Posey couldn't seem to stop herself from grinning

and kept giving Walter a thumbs-up and whispering about how awesome it had been to go up in that balloon.

Now, as Walter sat in silence in the car, watching farms and neighborhoods and gas stations whiz by, he could only think about one thing.

He had seen Tank's world.

Just like Tank had said he would.

That night, Walter sat in Tank's truck, holding the envelope with his name and address scrawled in Tank's messy handwriting.

He thought about being up there in Banjo's balloon and seeing Harmony below.

Hearing Tank say, "Ain't this something, little man? You and me seeing my world?"

Of course, he hadn't *really* heard Tank's voice.

That was impossible.

Still, Walter had this feeling that he couldn't shake.

This feeling that maybe he'd been wrong to think that Tank hadn't cared about Harmony.

He looked down at the envelope.

With shaky hands, he tore it open.

With a pounding heart, he took out the yellow lined paper and unfolded it.

Dear Walter,

I bet you're mad as anything at your chicken-hearted brother for not coming home to say goodbye before I went overseas.

I sure wouldn't blame you if you are.

Not one little bit.

But now I'm going to confess to you the truth, even if it takes me down a few pegs in your eyes.

I got on the bus in Fort Benning with my duffel bag and a heavy heart. And the closer I got to home, the heavier my heart felt just thinking about saying goodbye to Mama and Daddy, but most of all to you.

When that bus got halfway to Harmony, I told the driver to stop and let me off.

That's right. Your sorry ol' brother, Tank, was too chickenhearted to come home. I was afraid if I got back to Harmony, I might not ever want to leave again.

Ain't that a sorry thing to admit?

But no matter what, I want you to know that you and Harmony are my world.

So there you have it.

I hope you ain't too mad at me, little man.

Your chickenhearted brother,

Tank

FORTY-ONE

"Okay, what's rule number two?" Posey asked.

Walter sighed. They had been going over Caesar Romanoff's rules for making friends all morning, and frankly, he was bored.

But Posey was relentless.

"Rule number two?" she repeated a little testily.

"Look 'em in the eye and say their name," Walter said.

Posey nodded. "Perfect. Now here's one we haven't practiced yet. Rule number seven. Show sympathy. That's important. You don't have to actually cry or anything. Just *look* sad."

"Okay."

"Try it," Posey said. "Look sad."

Walter tried really hard to look sad, but he could tell that Posey wasn't satisfied.

Luckily, the unmistakable sound of Banjo's truck interrupted them.

Porkchop let out a snarl and barked.

"Banjo!" Walter called, racing out to Posey's mailbox, where Banjo's truck sputtered and rattled and coughed until it finally came to a stop.

They hadn't seen Banjo since the Macon County Key Grab four days ago. Walter's last glimpse of Banjo had been of him hobbling after Evalina's car, calling, "Wait! Evalina! Forgive me!"

And they hadn't seen hide nor hair of him until now.

When Banjo stepped out of the truck, Walter got the shock of his life.

The man who had stepped out of that truck sure didn't *look* like Banjo.

Instead of the greasy, dirt-stained overalls he usually wore, this new Banjo was wearing a suit.

But not just any suit.

A *white* suit.

And a vest.

A green velvet vest.

And a bow tie.

221

A green-and-white-striped bow tie.

And instead of his usual scraggly, too-long hair, this Banjo's hair was newly cut and neatly combed with a perfect part right down the middle.

That big twirly mustache was still there, but now it was trimmed and twirled to perfection.

Porkchop walked around and around Banjo, sniffing suspiciously and growling.

"Greetings and salutations," Banjo said, sweeping his arms out wide. "Feast your eyes upon the new and improved and *highly repentant* Jubilation T. Fairweather."

"Whoa!" Walter and Posey said at the exact same time.

"I trust my two young friends are faring well," he said. "I come bearing gifts."

He reached into the pocket of his jacket and pulled out two candy bars, presenting them with a flourish to Walter and Posey.

Posey made a face. "Really?" she said.

The candy bars looked more than a little old, their wrappers faded and dusty. Melted chocolate oozed out the sides.

"Um, thanks," Walter said, taking the candy bars and handing one to Posey.

Banjo reached behind him into the truck and pulled out the biggest bouquet of flowers Walter had ever seen.

"I have returned to win back the affections of the fair Evalina, my one and only true love," Banjo said. "For I find that I cannot bear to live another day on God's green earth without doing so."

"Oh, *puh-leese*," Posey said, wiping melted chocolate on the seat of her shorts.

"Out of my way, Miss Posey," Banjo said as he hobbled toward the porch steps.

Before he reached the top step, Evalina burst out of the screen door and said, "Don't bother, Banjo!"

"But I—" Banjo held the flowers with both hands and gazed up at Evalina.

"You nearly killed my one and only child and now you've got the gumption to show your face on my front porch?" Evalina let the screen door slam behind her and glared down at Banjo.

Walter could only stare in sheer amazement as Banjo began to work his magic on Evalina.

He proclaimed himself the biggest fool who had ever walked the face of the earth.

He exclaimed how he was lower than the lowly worms that slither in the mud and sorrier than the sorriest of the sorry.

He explained how he had let his curse of a temper take over his body and soul and cause pain and misery to the one and only person he had ever truly loved.

"That person is you, dear Evalina," he said. "You and only you."

Then he announced that he had seen the light.

He most assuredly realized the magnitude of his previously ignoble ways.

And last of all, he promised that standing here before them was a brand-new Jubilation T. Fairweather.

"I will remain your humble servant until my dying day," he said.

With that, he grew silent, holding those flowers and looking at Evalina with the most repentant eyes Walter had ever seen.

While Evalina stood there silently, eyes narrowed and toe tapping, Posey poked Walter. "Here's your chance to practice rule number seven," she whispered. "Pretend to show sympathy."

But Walter didn't have to pretend. He really did feel sympathy for Banjo. He hadn't won that shiny new truck he had been so sure he was going to win. His bodacious adventure had turned out to be anything but bodacious. And now Evalina was whopping mad at him.

The four of them stood there, still and quiet, until Evalina snatched the flowers out of Banjo's hand and yanked the screen door open.

"Oh, for heaven's sake," she said. "Come inside by the fan before you have a heatstroke in that ridiculous suit."

Banjo looked back at Walter and Posey and winked before following Evalina inside.

FORTY-TWO

Walter turned to Posey and said, "Tell me about some of the other books you had to leave behind in Tennessee."

They were sitting in Tank's truck, listening to country music on the radio, with Porkchop snoozing between them.

Posey didn't hesitate. She went on and on about those books.

"There was this one about how to plant a rainbow garden," she said. "Like purple beans and blue potatoes and things like that."

"Wow!" Walter said.

"There was another one that had about a million science experiments for kids. Like making a cannon with a cork and a soda bottle. And cool things with burning candles and magnets and stuff."

"No way!" Walter said.

"Yes way. I should've kept that one," she said.

She rattled on about some of the other books and didn't seem to even notice that Walter was practicing Caesar Romanoff's rules for making friends.

Then, just like in rule number two, Walter looked Posey right in the eye and said, "Posey."

He was nervous about what he was going to say next. He was going to use rule number six about flattery.

"I appreciate you helping me learn these rules for making friends," he said. "I know you're really good at 'em and I'm gonna watch you when we start school next week and do everything that you do."

Posey's face suddenly grew pale.

She looked down at her hands. "Well, um—" Her voice was quiet and a little trembly. "I might have a confession to make."

Walter was surprised at this new Posey, acting so timid and nervous. "What kind of confession?" he said.

Posey kept her eyes on her fidgeting fingers. "Um, I've never actually *used* any of Caesar Romanoff's rules for making friends," she said.

Walter's eyebrows shot up. "You haven't?"

Posey shook her head.

"Why not?" Walter asked.

Posey shrugged. "Too scared, I guess."

Scared?

Posey scared?

Walter couldn't even imagine that.

"Scared of what?" he said.

Posey lifted her head and looked at Walter.

"Scared of being noticed more than I already am, I guess," she said.

"Oh."

"When you got a face like mine," Posey said, "you get noticed plenty as it is. And not in a good way. I guess I always figured if I waltzed around looking kids in the eye and flattering them, well, I don't know . . ." She looked down at her hands again. "I just never did."

"So then, what about making friends?" Walter said.

"I never make any friends."

Walter didn't know what to say.

Was this really that same scabby-kneed girl who had hollered "Can't you read?" at him that day on the porch when they first met?

Was this that confident Posey, marching through the

woods in rubber boots, spouting all those nuggets of knowledge?

Was this that feisty girl with her feisty three-legged dog who had told Banjo to have fun at his pity party? That girl with grit and fortitude?

Was this the girl who had had that bodacious adventure with him?

"I have an idea," Walter said.

Posey fiddled with her fingers and waited.

"When we get to school, let's use Caesar Romanoff's rules together," he said.

"Together?"

"Yeah, you know, when we walk down the hall and stuff. Or in the cafeteria."

"I don't know," Posey said.

Walter grabbed her by the shoulders, making Porkchop wake up and growl a little.

"Rule number one," Walter said. "Think positive."

Posey smiled.

A very small smile, but still, a smile.

"Okay. I'll try," she said.

Walter let go of her shoulders and looked out the window of the truck. "Now *I* have a confession," he said.

Posey cocked her head.

"Tank was up there in that balloon with me," Walter said.

Posey's eyes grew wide.

"I know what you're thinking. You're thinking I must be nuts."

"No, I'm not."

"You're not?"

Posey shook her head. "I'm not."

"I know he wasn't *really* there," Walter went on. "I mean, not there like I could see him or touch him or anything. But he was there. And I saw his world, just like in my dream."

"You did?"

Walter nodded. "And it was Harmony. Tank's world was Harmony."

Walter took Tank's letter out of the glove box and let Posey read it.

When she was finished, she wiped at her teary eyes and said, "That's so sweet." She handed the letter back to Walter. "Your brother was nice."

Walter nodded. "Yeah. And you wanna know what else?"

"What?"

"The last time I had that dream, I blew out all the candles."

"Really?"

"I haven't had that dream since then," Walter said. "And I know I'm *not* going to have it again. I just know it."

Posey nodded. "Makes sense to me," she said.

"I'm thinking maybe that dream was just a little blip of feel-good like you said."

Posey looked at Walter with wide eyes. "No," she said. "It was more than that. It was Tank sending you a message through that dream."

"A message?"

Posey nodded.

A message.

Yes! A message. Tank had wanted Walter to know how much he loved Harmony.

And then Banjo's Bodacious Adventure had come along to help Walter understand.

Who would've ever thought *that* would happen?

Walter and Posey sat there not talking for a while.

Just listening to Tank's favorite country music station on the radio, with Porkchop snuggled on Posey's lap.

Walter leaned his head back against the seat and closed his eyes.

School would be starting in two days.

Usually his stomach would be churning with dread at the thought of it.

But now the most amazing thing was happening.

Walter's stomach was fluttering with excitement.

Not a big flutter.

But still, a flutter.

He could picture it now.

Him and Posey strutting down the halls of Harmony Elementary School, kindred spirits practicing Caesar Romanoff's rules for making friends.

Tank sure would have been proud.